Giving ⬛⬛⬛⬛ **make**
it that ⬛⬛⬛
against ⬛⬛⬛ **barn**

Ruth Ann le⬛⬛ ⬛ack, pulling away from his mesmerizing kiss. His hold loosened, but instead of stopping, he took the kisses from her lips to her cheeks, her eyes and her chin, which was almost as devastating.

"It's okay," he murmured. "You're safe. I've got you."

"No." She took a deep breath. "You don't." Pushing him, she managed a step backward. And another, breaking the circle of his arms.

Jonah stood motionless, staring at her. Finally he took a deep breath and straightened. "You're right. The situation is complicated and what just happened didn't make anything better. My apologies." Walking past her, he left the stall. Moments later she heard a truck engine start.

She simply couldn't afford to leave herself vulnerable where Jonah Granger was concerned.

Dear Reader,

Like many little girls, I enjoyed a love affair with horses. I read *Black Beauty* and also loved historical novels, where the characters went everywhere on horseback or in carriages. Like most teenagers, however, I eventually got busy with homework and boys, and my horse obsession died away.

Or so I thought. When my own daughter wanted to ride, I drove her to the stable. While glancing around at the pastures, I was hit by a wave of intense longing. The stable owner walked up, we introduced ourselves and I said, "Can I ride, too?"

That was almost eight years ago. These days I'm the devoted caretaker of five horses and twenty-two acres of land. I believed I'd left my junior high school dreams of a life with horses behind. Now I can't imagine living without them.

The heroine of *Smoky Mountain Home*, Ruth Ann Blakely, shares my passion for horses. She's also passionate about Jonah Granger—passionately opposed to his plan to replace her beloved, historic stable with a new equestrian center. Yet she's desperately in love with the man himself. Does Ruth Ann have to sacrifice her past in order to have a future with Jonah?

I hope you enjoy spending time with Ruth Ann, Jonah and all the horse characters I had fun creating for this story. I love to hear from readers—please feel free to contact me at my Web site, www.lynnette-kent.com, or by letter in care of Harlequin American Romance.

Happy reading!

Lynnette Kent

Smoky Mountain Home
LYNNETTE KENT

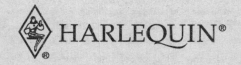

TORONTO • NEW YORK • LONDON
AMSTERDAM • PARIS • SYDNEY • HAMBURG
STOCKHOLM • ATHENS • TOKYO • MILAN • MADRID
PRAGUE • WARSAW • BUDAPEST • AUCKLAND

ISBN-13: 978-0-373-75231-7
ISBN-10:   0-373-75231-8

SMOKY MOUNTAIN HOME

ABOUT THE AUTHOR

Lynnette Kent began writing her first romance in the fourth grade, about a ship's stowaway who would fall in love with her captain, Christopher Columbus. Years of scribbling later, her husband suggested she write one of those "Harlequin romances" she loved to read. With his patience and her two daughters' support, Lynnette realized her dream of being a published novelist. She now lives in North Carolina, where she divides her time between books—writing and reading—and the horses she adores. Feel free to contact Lynnette via her Web site, www.lynnette-kent.com or write her at P.O. Box 1012, Vass, NC 28394.

Books by Lynnette Kent

For Angela,
consummate horsewoman and incomparable friend

Chapter One

Jonah Granger was exactly what she'd expected.

His straight black hair had been styled into a perfect tousle, no doubt at a salon in New York City which had charged two hundred dollars for the privilege. He wore gray flannel slacks with a dark-brown turtleneck sweater, probably cashmere, and managed to look artistic but still businesslike while showing off his strong, square shoulders and his flat belly. Add in Italian loafers and a discreet, hideously expensive gold watch. Everything about the man screamed class and money.

Ruth Ann Blakely gritted her teeth as she watched the architect explain his design, and watched The Hawkridge School's board of directors melt under the warmth of his smile. Even Jayne Thomas, their usually pragmatic headmistress, seemed swept away by the grandiose plans displayed on Jonah Granger's easel.

"Thirty-foot ceilings," he was saying, "for air circulation and light, with a series of archways creating unique visual effects."

"Like a Gothic cathedral." Board chairwoman Miriam Edwards sighed. "How wonderful."

Ruth Ann rolled her eyes.

"Exactly," Granger said, aiming the spotlight of his attention right at Miriam. "The clerestory windows provide ventilation in the summer and a solar-heating effect in the winter."

"Smart." Harry Hopkins nodded. "Save on the heating bills."

Examining the backs of her hands, which testified to twenty-five or so winters spent working in an unheated stable, Ruth Ann bit her lower lip to keep from laughing.

"The stall floors will be textured concrete, but the aisles of the stable will be paved with brick."

Oh, no, they won't. Ruth Ann shifted in her chair. *My horses aren't spending their lives standing on concrete, not even if it's underneath the mats you haven't mentioned.*

"I've provided a lounge for parents and students." Granger flipped the page to reveal an artistic rendering of what looked like a nightclub. "Sofas for conversation, tables and chairs for meals prepared in the full-sized kitchen equipped with marble counter tops and professional appliances, plus a complete audio-video system."

Ruth Ann burst out laughing.

The thirteen board members sitting around the conference table turned to stare at her. Jonah Granger raised his straight black eyebrows and looked down the slope of his nose at her. "Is something funny?"

She tried to control herself, but whenever she glanced at the drawing, she couldn't help another cackle. "S-sorry," she said finally, wiping her eyes. "That's a—a really nice room."

"Thank—"

"If you're building a house or a hotel," she interrupted. "But my barn doesn't need so much—" she waved a hand "—stuff."

Those slashing brows moved higher. "*Your* barn?"

Jayne Thomas cleared her throat. "I didn't get a chance to introduce you, because Ms. Blakely arrived after the presentation started. Jonah Granger, this is Ruth Ann Blakely, The Hawkridge School's equestrian trainer and instructor."

"Ah." Jonah Granger sent her a cool nod. "Nice to meet you, Ms. Blakely. I'm sure we'll be able to work well together."

"I'm not." Ruth Ann got to her feet. "This so-called stable you've designed might be pretty, but it won't work for horses or their caretakers. On the other hand, the stable we use now was designed by people who understood the art and science of equines." She glanced around the conference table, making eye contact with the few board members who weren't pretending to study their notes. "All *my* barn needs is some renovation and restoration to make it as good as new. If you'd like to discuss those possibilities, Mr. Granger, I'll be more than happy to talk with you. But I'm not signing off on a new barn that's more about looking good in the parent brochure than about caring for the animals and giving the girls safe, productive lessons."

She left the conference room by the nearest door, and congratulated herself for not tripping or running into a chair on her way out. Sometimes her feet forgot their main job, especially when she was nervous. Facing down Jonah Granger had definitely made her nervous. He was so cool, so controlled, so…

"Arrogant," she muttered as she reached the grand circular staircase descending to the first floor. "Contemptuous. Conceited." Her riding boots sounded like the horses themselves as she hurried down the marble steps. "Egotis—"

She stopped moving and muttering as she rounded the curve and saw a girl sitting on the bottom step. "Hello, there. Can I help you?"

The girl turned to look at her as she came the rest of the way to ground level. "No, thank you. I'm just waiting." She would be about thirteen, with dark hair pulled back at the nape of her neck, a round face and a chubby body dressed in tank top and jeans a size too small.

"Waiting for what?" Ruth Ann leaned an elbow on the newel post. The fall semester didn't start for another week, and all the students had left campus for a brief vacation.

"My stepfather." The girl stared straight ahead. "Mr. Granger."

"Ah." That might explain the odd air of withdrawal, as if she'd walled herself off from the rest of the world. He'd be a demanding parent, which played hell with an adolescent's self-esteem, in Ruth Ann's experience. "I just left that meeting. He should be finished in a few minutes."

A nod was the only response. But then, with a sideways glance at her breeches and boots, the girl said, "You ride? Horses?"

"I'm the trainer here. Do you ride?"

"Oh, no." She shook her head. "I mean, I do, kinda. But it's really scary."

"Maybe you haven't had the right horse. What's your name?"

After hesitating a moment, she said, "Darcy."

Ruth Ann offered a handshake. "I'm Ruth Ann Blakely. Good to meet you, Darcy."

Jonah Granger hadn't taught his stepdaughter how to shake properly. She barely grazed Ruth Ann's palm with her own, then let her arm fall back to her lap.

The approach of voices from upstairs announced that the meeting had ended. Darcy jerked her head up, got to her feet, and scurried to the other side of the entry hall, like a mouse caught on the counter when the kitchen light comes on.

Ruth Ann's temper started to simmer again. What had the man done to make this girl so nervous?

Flanked by board members, Jonah Granger came down the stairs, carrying his big box of useless drawings and smiling at the compliments of people who wouldn't know a hoof pick from a hay hook. At the bottom, he spoke with each and every one of them as they left by the front door, before finally deigning to notice his stepdaughter.

"Darcy, there you are." He grinned at the girl and summoned her with a gesture. "I thought you'd still be in the library."

To Ruth Ann's surprise, Darcy moved quickly to join him. "I didn't feel like reading. I went for a walk instead."

He put his hand on her shoulder. "Did you like what you saw?"

The girl shrugged. "It's pretty."

"When you come back to start classes," Jayne Thomas said, "you'll get an extensive tour, and you can see how beautiful Hawkridge really is. We have hiking paths on the mountain and, of course, the riding trails." The lift of her eyebrow in Ruth Ann's direction promised a reprimand as soon as they had a private moment.

But Ruth Ann was more interested in the fact that Darcy would be attending Hawkridge. "Maybe you'd like to sign up for some lessons," she told the girl. "I promise to keep you safe, and you'll have a good time."

Jonah Granger's smile vanished. "Darcy's had her fill of horseback accidents, I believe. But she's an excellent pianist, and plays several other instruments, too."

The teenager gazed at her toes, their nails painted a glittery blue.

"She'll have lots of choices," Jayne promised, with a warning glance at Ruth Ann, who had opened her mouth to protest. "And lots of time to decide what she wants to do." Setting a hand lightly on Granger's shoulder, she ushered him toward the door. "You'll be coming in from New York next week—"

Aha! Ruth Ann thought.

"—to bring Darcy for Moving-In Day. Let's arrange another meeting then. We can review your plans in more detail. Ruth Ann will give us her input at that time."

From the double doorway, Jonah Granger threw Ruth Ann a glance that could have been called challenging. Or just spitting mad.

"I'll look forward to it," he told the headmistress, his voice as smooth as black ice.

Jayne went outside with Granger and Darcy. Staying within the shadows, Ruth Ann peeked around the door frame in time to see the architect and his daughter fold themselves into a dark-blue Porsche. With a roar of the engine and a squeal of tires, the sports car streaked around the circular drive.

"Showoff," Ruth Ann muttered. "Just what I'd expect."

Jayne remained on the front steps until the forest surrounding them hid the Porsche from sight. Returning to the entry hall, she closed the doors and stood for a moment facing the carved mahogany panels, holding onto the big brass handles.

Ruth Ann decided not to wait for the lecture to start. "Look, I'm sorry I was late. I scheduled the vet visit for one o'clock three months ago, but he had an emergency and didn't arrive until after two. I couldn't just walk off and leave him with six horses to handle on his own. Nobody consulted me when they set up this meeting." She gave a disgusted sniff. "Not surprising. The board would probably have preferred I never show up at all."

"Especially when you started talking." Jayne crossed the marble-tiled entry hall and entered the school's office suite. "Let's go to my office and sit down."

Once they'd settled into the chairs on either side of Jayne's big desk, she shook her head. "Your opposition to the new stable doesn't make a lot of sense, Ruth Ann. Why wouldn't you want a new building with all the amenities? Surely an up-to-date facility would make your job easier?"

Ruth Ann propped her elbows on the armrests and stared at her linked fingers as she constructed the answer in her head.

"Why don't we tear down the Manor and build a new, state-of-the-art classroom building? We could have computer hookups at every seat, modern labs for the science classes, high-tech recordings for the language teachers, an auditorium *and* a dining room and—"

Laughing, Jayne held up a hand. "Enough, already. I agree—there's a great deal of historic value in all of the buildings on the estate, including the stable." She took a deep breath and slowly blew it out again. "The board—"

"Meaning Miriam Edwards."

"The board," Jayne repeated firmly, "believes the current facility is unsafe for the students."

Ruth Ann characterized that opinion with a single rude word.

"Maybe," Jayne conceded with a tilt of her head. "We've never had an accident involving the building itself. And," she said before Ruth Ann could, "we've never had a girl seriously hurt while riding. You're a great trainer and instructor, Ruth Ann. You're a terrific therapist—you and your horses have made a real difference for a number of girls the rest of us had just about given up on." The Hawkridge School served as a refuge and, often, a last resort for girls whose emotional problems had driven them into troublesome, even dangerous, behavior.

Blinking hard, Ruth Ann said, "I'm glad. I love my job."

"Good. What we're going to have to do is find some way to compromise on the stable. I don't know what that means, yet, except that you'll need to cooperate with Jonah Granger as he works on the design."

"Why can't he design a renovation?" Ruth Ann sat

forward in her chair. "The old barn needs some work, some updating, sure. Can't Granger simply fix what's wrong and leave what's right?"

"That's not what he does."

"Then find someone who will."

"The board wants Granger. He built a house and barn for Miriam's sister up in Connecticut, and she's just wild about his work."

"So let him build something new for her. He can leave my barn alone."

Jayne's brown eyes were kind, but she said, "It's not actually *your* barn, Ruth Ann."

"My dad took care of it until the day he died. Literally— his heart stopped while he was sweeping the aisle that night."

"I know."

"My grandfather and his father before him worked in that barn taking care of the estate's horses. How am I supposed to walk away from that?"

"It's just stone and wood, sweetie. You and the horses are what matters. Those would be the same in a new stable."

"I don't think so." Ruth Ann got to her feet. "Call me superstitious or just plain weird, but my barn is a special place. The horses know it and the girls know it—the ones who really care, anyway. Moving the equestrian program to a new stable would be a mistake."

Jayne stood up. "As a friend, I'm asking you to cooperate. Please…for my sake?"

Ruth Ann frowned at her. "Unfair." Then she sighed. "Okay. For your sake, I will listen to what he has to say. Are you going to ask him to do the same?"

"Of course."

"For all the good that will do," Ruth Ann muttered, once

she'd closed the office door between herself and the headmistress. "I'll bet my bottom dollar that Jonah Granger listens to no one's opinion but his own!"

RUTH ANN BLAKELY was not what he'd anticipated.

Jonah admitted he'd been expecting someone like his ex-wife, Darcy's mother—slim and neat, with polished boots, hair combed into a sleek ponytail and a lipstick smile. More, he'd expected to be listened to, consulted, and then given the go-ahead on the stable project.

Instead, she'd laughed at him, dammit. Made fun of his plans. He simply couldn't believe it. What did *she* know about architecture, anyway? She spent her days mucking out stalls and teaching kids to ride. Who did she think she was, criticizing his work?

He'd known she was trouble as soon as she entered the conference room—*late,* to begin with—after Jayne Thomas had introduced him and he'd started his presentation. Her skepticism, her resistance to his project, had surrounded her like a force field. He doubted a word he'd said had gotten through.

She certainly hadn't gone to any trouble to impress him. She'd stalked in wearing riding breeches, dusty boots and a T-shirt with a huge green smear across the front, as if some horse had used her for its napkin. Face shaded by the baseball cap she hadn't taken off, her damp ponytail drooping through the hole in the back, she'd conveyed quite clearly that he was interrupting her important work. As she'd stomped out again, he'd noticed that she was tall, well built on generous lines, and furious.

Well, that made two of them.

Darcy stirred in the seat beside him, and Jonah realized he should be talking with her instead of silently venting his frustrations. "So what did you think of the school?"

She shrugged one shoulder. "It's okay."

He refused to be daunted. "The Hawkridge estate was built in the early 1900s as a wealthy businessman's personal home. His daughter turned it into a school in the 1960s."

His stepdaughter yawned. "Looks like a castle. Maybe it's haunted."

Jonah chuckled. "Maybe." When she didn't say anything else, he tried again. "I thought the headmistress was pleasant. She doesn't seem like the type to be hiding instruments of torture in her office."

After a long silence, Darcy said, "The riding teacher was nice."

So much for diverting his thoughts from the belligerent Ms. Blakely. "What did you talk about?"

"Riding. She said the right horse would make it less scary."

Nice of her, giving an opinion on something she knew nothing about. On the other hand, Darcy needed all the encouragement she could get. "Maybe you can do some riding when you're at school."

"Mom told me I was useless around horses."

"Your mother…" Jonah clamped down on the impulse to speak his mind concerning his ex-wife. "She was upset that day, Darcy. You'd just fallen off and broken your arm. The horse was still running loose. You know she didn't mean what she said."

He glanced over, and saw that Darcy's long-fingered hands were clamped into fists in her lap. "She said it later, too. While they were putting the cast on my arm."

"Damn her." This time the curse erupted before he could stop it. He couldn't believe even Brittany would be so cruel to her own daughter. Brittany, of course, hadn't bothered to confess what she'd said until a month later, while they sat on opposite sides of the emergency room waiting for the doctors to pump half a bottle of pain pills out of Darcy's stomach.

He cleared his throat. "Sorry. Obviously, I have some serious problems with your mother, or else I'd still be married to her." He wanted to share a smile with Darcy, but she was staring out the window. "You're with me now, so don't worry about getting hassled like that anymore."

She didn't turn around. Finally, though, she murmured, "The teachers..."

"The teachers at Hawkridge are there to help you, and not just with schoolwork. They're more like friends you can count on to listen and support you when you're having problems." He hoped so, anyway, for Darcy's sake. No thirteen-year-old girl should be desperate enough to attempt suicide.

His stomach rumbled, and Jonah switched to a more cheerful topic. "It's been a long afternoon and I'm starving. How do you feel about pizza for supper? I hear there's a pretty good place in town. We could stop there before we go back to the hotel."

Darcy gave him another of those defeated shrugs. "Pizza's fattening."

More of her mother's wisdom, no doubt. "We'll walk around town afterwards, look in the shop windows and work off the calories." His stepdaughter didn't answer. "Or we could go swimming in the hotel's heated pool."

"I can't wear a swimsuit."

"Darcy..." Jonah started to protest, but pulled himself up short. He wasn't sure what the right response would be—as the only child of two only children, he lacked the sisters and female cousins who might have provided experience. His instincts about women were obviously lousy, otherwise he would never have gotten involved with Brittany...or Cindi or Annelise or Jacqueline...in the first place.

At least Brittany was the only mistake he'd married.

"Well," he said, braking as they approached the town limit of Ridgeville, "most pizza restaurants offer salads, too. But I hope you'll have a piece or two of the pizza. Otherwise, I'll have to eat the whole thing myself. And then I'll have to walk for hours to work it off. I might not get to sleep tonight."

He thought he heard a snort of amusement from Darcy. He'd take that as progress.

But he hoped The Hawkridge School could do better. And he prayed that Jayne Thomas and her staff would show him how to avoid making mistakes with this fragile soul for whom he'd taken responsibility. Now that Brittany had transferred custody to him, he planned to move to Ridgeville within the next few weeks. Living nearby, and without his ex-wife's constant interference, Jonah hoped he could learn to be the parent Darcy needed.

Business-wise, planning and construction of the school's stable, along with his other projects in Atlanta and Charlotte, would allow him to start up his solo firm in North Carolina on a solid financial basis. Without the Hawkridge commission, though, he couldn't cover his expenses. He'd have to spend another year in New York, working with his prima-donna boss and going not-so-quietly insane.

So whether she knew it or not, Ms. Ruth Ann Blakely held his future in her hands. If he didn't win her support on the stable, he wouldn't be his own boss for at least another year. More important, he wouldn't be able to give Darcy the support he knew she needed.

But the argumentative, assertive Ms. Blakely would not be easy to win over. And given his lousy track record with women, Jonah didn't have a clue what approach to take!

Chapter Two

Someone had set fire to the sky.

Or so it looked to Ruth Ann, studying the sunrise during her walk from her cottage, on the main campus, to the stable. Red-gold clouds hovered just above the treeline, reflecting pink light onto the mist rising off the mountains.

"Red sky in morning, sailor take warning," she told herself. "I wonder if that still holds true when we're four hundred miles inland and a mile above sea level."

Two hours later, with her horses fed but half the stalls still needing to be cleaned, she propped her chin on her hands, gripped around the handle of a manure fork, and gazed at the gentle rain falling outside the barn windows. "I guess it is true. We're going to have rain for Moving-In Day."

Waldo, the twenty-three year old Percheron, stuck his huge white head over his stall door and whickered in her direction. Ruth Ann moved closer to rub the soft white hair on his cheeks and throat. "No time for a ride today, old man. I'll be down at the school until dinnertime, helping the girls get settled."

He pushed his nose into her hand, and she knuckled the velvety pink skin between his nostrils. "Yes, even in the rain.

We're all gonna be chilled and damp by the end of the afternoon. I hope they're planning spaghetti for dinner."

The horse lipped her fingers. "This new cook makes some strange choices, though. She served spinach quiche for lunch one day during summer school—whatever made her think teenagers who'd spent the morning hiking and swimming in the summer heat would want eggs and spinach for lunch? What do you suppose Cook thought when most of the pieces of her green and yellow pie returned to the kitchen untouched?"

Lightning flashed outside, followed quickly by the growl of thunder. Waldo turned away and paced to the outside door of his stall, settling in to contemplate the weather.

"Just as well," Ruth Ann murmured to herself, and to the horses around her as she hurried to finish her work. "I've got to be at the dorm by nine. I hope there are more dads here this year than last. I really don't want to spend all morning schlepping luggage in the rain."

Just in case, though, she donned her raincoat and pulled rubber boots over her sneakers. She checked the various buckets set under the leaks in the roof and emptied those more than a third full.

"That'll hold us till lunchtime," she told Patsy, a dark bay thoroughbred mare. "I'll rush back while the girls and their folks are eating. Be good."

The Hawkridge stables were located half a mile from the main house and the dormitories, an easy walk across the lawns and meadows of the grounds. Driving her pickup truck to avoid the rain required Ruth Ann to use the four-mile service road running through the forest surrounding the estate. Here and there, the trees were starting to show a few yellow-edged leaves and some splotches of red. After a hot, dry summer, the welcome rain had already washed away lots of dust, leaving the woods a deep green against which the autumn colors glowed brightly.

Due to the weather, parents would be unloading their cars as close to the dorm as possible, so Ruth Ann left her truck in the faculty parking lot near the main house—the Manor, Howard Ridgely had called it, a title that had stuck—and walked to the more modern student residence behind. Inside, the usual controlled chaos of Moving-In Day ruled. Because the girls on each grade level roomed together on a hallway, all students would be relocating today, whether this was their first year at Hawkridge or not.

Alice Tolbert, the head of the literature department, sat at a table on one side of the big room, checking in first-time students. Across the open space leading from the front door to the staircase, the new physics teacher, Teresa James, occupied the table where returning students would pick up their room assignments. Having just graduated from college herself, Teresa was still making the adjustment from student to authority figure.

Ruth Ann went to stand beside her. "How's it going?"

Brushing shiny blond bangs back from her face, Teresa produced a tense smile. "I think I'm doing this right. I've had a few complaints, though."

"Someone's always going to be unhappy with their new room." Ruth Ann pulled up a chair and sat down. "They complained last year, they'll complain next year. Just ignore it."

The physics teacher glanced around. "I want them to like me," she said in a low voice. "I've heard I'm replacing the most popular teacher in the school." Then she winced. "I mean, you're a teacher and I'm sure they all like you—"

"Don't worry." Ruth Ann grinned. "Mason Reed was definitely popular—he was the only male, he's handsome as sin and a really nice guy. But now he's in Boston with his new wife, starting classes in engineering himself, God bless him. And we are going to carry on just fine without him." She nodded at the girl who came to the table. "Hi, Sherry, good to see you. This is Ms. James, the new physics teacher. And your room this year will be…"

The morning passed quickly. Ruth Ann stuck by Teresa James until the young teacher seemed to feel more at ease. Then she helped new students convey bags and boxes to their rooms, making conversation to ease the difficult moments. Most parents bringing their daughters to Hawkridge carried with them some kind of guilt or a sense of failure. The girls themselves were often resentful as well as scared—they'd been brought to this school because they couldn't be trusted to follow the rules anywhere else. And Hawkridge rules were tough—no alcohol, cigarettes, drugs or sex, no piercings, no makeup or jewelry other than a watch, no unescorted trips off-campus.

Of course, not all girls complied with all of the rules. But the success rate at Hawkridge was high. Most students left with a good sense of self-esteem and real, reachable goals for their lives. Ruth Ann took pride in the part her horses played in that process.

As she returned to the lounge after carrying a heavy pair of suitcases to the fourth floor, she saw Darcy Granger standing in the midst of the traffic flowing through the room. Clutching a bed pillow in a pink cover against her chest, she looked completely bewildered, on the verge of tears.

Had her stepfather dropped her off without making sure she got where she belonged? Jonah Granger was probably worried his Porsche would be hit by one of the other parents' cars.

Ruth Ann approached Darcy. "Hey, there. I'm glad to see you made it. Have you checked in yet?"

Darcy shook her head, her eyes wide and her lips pursed as she stared at the bustle around her.

"Okay, then, you come stand here." With a light hand on Darcy's shoulder, Ruth Ann led the girl to the check-in line. "Is your da— Is Mr. Granger coming back?"

"I think so."

"Good. He'll see you if you stay in the line." Ruth Ann looked around for other girls who needed help, but this late in the morning, almost everyone had arrived. Lunch in the Manor dining hall with their parents would be the opening of the school year. Then would come all the tearful—and quite a few not-so-tearful—goodbyes.

Alice Tolbert was talking to Darcy, going over papers and forms in a gentle voice. And still Jonah Granger hadn't made an appearance. Ruth Ann heaved a big sigh, shrugged into the slicker she'd discarded a couple of hours ago, and went out into the rain to find him.

What she found first was a mountain of luggage right outside the front door. She counted ten suitcases, four large and four medium plus two huge athletic bags, stuffed until the seams had started to pull. Each was labeled with a lime-green luggage tag which read Darcy Granger.

As she stared at the pile, a man came around the corner of the building nearest the parking lot, wheeling a handcart on which rested a full-sized footlocker—the kind the military issued for recruits to store all of their gear. This one was shiny black, with silver metal on the corners, and Ruth Ann had a feeling that—even if she hadn't recognized Jonah Granger's tall, lean frame—this, too, would have Darcy's name on it.

When Granger reached the bottom of the steps he stopped, straightened up and blew out a long breath. Then he glanced up and saw Ruth Ann.

"This is the last of her gear," he said, his voice even, emotionless. "If you'll point the way to the elevator inside, I'll get everything to her room."

Ruth Ann struggled with the smile she knew would only infuriate him. "I'm afraid we don't use the elevator on Moving-In Day. It's only for emergencies."

He leaned an elbow on the upturned edge of the footlocker. "You're kidding, right?"

She shook her head. "Afraid not." Today, he wore jeans and boat shoes and a leather jacket softened with wear—but not too much—in all the right places. His wet hair had fallen into very natural and appealing spikes across his tanned forehead, and his long eyelashes had caught several beads of water. Did the man ever look less than gorgeous?

His blue gaze remained locked on her face for a moment, the expression changing from surprise to irritation to a steely resolve. "Okay, then. No problem." Grabbing the handle of the handcart, he began to bump it up the steps. When he reached the top, Ruth Ann opened the door for him to back through.

"Thanks," he said, without looking at her.

When she came inside again, he was standing with Darcy and Alice, getting an explanation of where Darcy's room would be. He glanced at Ruth Ann, and lifted an eyebrow. "You don't have to carry those. We'll manage."

Ruth Ann would have shrugged, but the two athletic bags were slung over her shoulders and in each hand she held a large suitcase. "That's what I'm here for. And you haven't got much time—lunch is at noon. Which room, Alice?"

"Two East, Fourteen," Alice said, meaning the east wing of the second floor, room fourteen.

"That's a good one," Ruth Ann told Darcy as they started up the steps. "You'll get morning sunshine and cool afternoons."

Darcy didn't answer. Behind them, her stepfather bumped the footlocker up a step at a time.

As they walked down the hallway, Ruth Ann could see that the door to room fourteen stood open. "Your roommate must be here already. Did Ms. Tolbert tell you her name?"

Darcy shrugged one shoulder. "Um…Eve, I think."

One step over the threshold, however, she stopped dead and actually shrank back. Ruth Ann unloaded the luggage she carried outside the room, next to the wall, and then peered around Darcy to see what the problem might be. A mother and daughter occupied the room's two chairs, the younger practically a mirror image of the older—fashionably thin, wearing designer jeans, shoes and tops, their faces perfectly made up, ash-blond hair perfectly styled.

Confronted by the double dose of chic, Ruth Ann suddenly felt like the ugly green giant. As an adult, however, she was required to handle the situation, not run away from it.

Clearing her throat, she said, "Hi, Eve. This is Darcy Granger. She'll be your roommate." Moving Darcy further into the room with a gentle push, she offered a hand to Eve's mother. "I'm Ruth Ann Blakely, the equestrian trainer at Hawkridge."

Limp fingers brushed briefly against hers. "Nina Forrest."

Eve's expression didn't change. She barely glanced at Darcy. "Hi."

Nina looked beyond Ruth Ann. "And you are…?" she purred.

"Darcy's stepfather, Jonah." He reached past Ruth Ann for a handshake, nudging her arm in the process. She fought a surprising urge to shy from his touch like a startled horse.

Nina Forrest had no such qualms and offered him a feline smile along with her hand. "It's good to meet you, Jonah. I've heard about your work, of course. Who in New York hasn't?"

"Thanks." Letting go of Nina, he looked at Eve. "It's good to meet you, Eve."

Her smile was as predatory as her mother's. "Thank you, Jonah."

Ruth Ann drew in a deep breath, half annoyance, half surprise at the girl's lack of respect. Before she could say anything, though, a bell chimed twice in the hallway.

"That's the lunch bell," she told the two girls and their parents. "You've got five minutes to get to the dining hall."

As the four of them left the room, Jonah Granger looked at Ruth Ann. "I need to get the rest of Darcy's bags. Could you take her to the lunch room and I'll—"

She shook her head at him. "Nope. You two go on to the dining hall," she ordered, emphasizing the last two words. Hawkridge possessed nothing as mundane as a lunch room. "I'll carry up the rest of the bags."

"You can't bring all those big bags up the stairs," he protested.

"I won't." Ruth Ann grinned. "I'll use the elevator."

"But—" He glared at her. "You said—"

"I'm staff." She pushed him toward the exit in Nina Forrest's wake. "There are some rules I get to break."

DARCY felt sick to her stomach, so she took an extra roll when the plate got passed to her. Food made her feel better.

Her roommate ignored the rolls. And the lasagna, the applesauce and the milk. She took some salad when the bowl came by and poured herself a glass of water from the pitcher in the center of the table. Eve refused dessert, too—chocolate cake with vanilla ice cream—and she only ate half of the salad on her plate. No wonder her waist was the size of a pencil.

Eve's mother ate the same way—salad and water. At least she had the excuse that she never stopped talking to Jonah long enough to chew. Jonah, meanwhile, had gone into defensive mode. He knew how to deflect women like Eve's mom with smiles and nods that made her believe he listened to every word, while in fact he was thinking about something else, probably a building design. Darcy had seen him deal with her mother that way. Before the fighting got really bad.

Looking around, Darcy noticed that the parents at most tables seemed to be talking to each other, but the girls didn't say much. It wasn't like the beginning of the year at a regular school, where you were glad to get back with your friends…if you had any. Hawkridge was a school for girls with "issues." As far as Darcy was concerned, parents seemed to be the real reason kids had issues to begin with. So it made sense they wouldn't talk to their parents.

This lunch was really kinda painful, though. She would have liked it better if they'd just let Jonah say goodbye and abandon her to her fate.

The chocolate cake was delicious, so Darcy took a second helping while the headmistress was giving her welcome speech. If they had meals like this three times a day, plus decent teachers, maybe Hawkridge wouldn't be so bad. Darcy could face almost anything, with good books and good food.

Well, except for her mother.

"You have fifteen minutes to get the last of your belongings into your rooms and say goodbye downstairs," the headmistress, Ms Thomas, said. "The student floors are now open to students and staff only. Parents, we'll be starting our program here at Hawkridge at 2:00 p.m. and you'll be on your way home. Have a safe trip!"

Everybody stood and started to leave the big dining hall. Eve's mother turned to Jonah.

"Let me give you my card," she said, with the smile that

reminded Darcy of a hungry panther. "I represent some very nice properties in Lower Manhattan, Chelsea, Tribeca—you might find yourself looking for a new place to live, now that Daisy is in school here."

Jonah took the card between two fingers. "Darcy," he corrected. "I will be relocating, as a matter of fact. To this area," he continued, when Nina started to say something. "While I'm involved with projects around the southeast. But—" He gave her his smooth, won't-happen grin. "I'll call if I need something."

Judging by Nina's smile, she expected a call tonight. "Please do." Then she turned to Eve. "Come on, darling. Kiss Mummy goodbye."

Darcy saw Jonah roll his eyes as he turned away. He put a hand on her shoulder as they walked into the big entry hall and out onto the front steps. His palm felt warm, heavy in a nice way. That was just one of the good things about being with Jonah—he didn't mind holding hands, even giving hugs. Her mother, Darcy had learned early, didn't touch. Not little girls, anyway.

Standing a couple of steps down so they were pretty much eye to eye, Jonah looked at her. "I thought I'd get to help you unpack," he said, frowning. "Are you going to be able to handle it by yourself?"

Darcy blinked hard. "I guess so." She should be used to goodbyes, used to being alone. She'd survived most of the summer by herself, once her mother had left for Europe, until Jonah had found out and rescued her. The last few weeks with him had been a lot more fun.

So letting him go was hard. When she lived in her mother's house, at least she knew all the servants' names. Here, she knew nobody, except for Eve. Some comfort.

"Darcy?" Jonah tapped her lightly on the chin with his fist.

"I'm going to be around, you know—I've got a meeting about the stable tomorrow morning. I'll bet we can run into each other every time I'm out here, if we work it right."

He looked worried, and she didn't want him to worry. "Sure," she said, working up a smile. "I'll look for you between classes tomorrow."

"Great. I—"

"Hey, Darcy, there you are!"

She turned around to see Ms. Blakely standing in the doorway.

"You'd better hurry," she said, beckoning for Darcy to join her. "You definitely don't want to be the last one to sit down— that means you have to stand up first to introduce yourself to the school."

Looking back at Jonah, Darcy found him grinning. "Go on." He nodded. "I'll see you soon."

Should she give him a hug? With a teacher watching? Did he care? Darcy wasn't sure.

Then he leaned over and kissed her cheek. "Be safe," he whispered.

Darcy nodded. "Bye." She ran up the steps and past Ms. Blakely, who pointed her toward the dining hall. A few girls were still coming down the big circular staircase, so she hustled ahead of them and managed to grab a chair in time. She wasn't going to be the last to sit or the first to say her name.

No way was she starting out at a new school as a geek!

JONAH watched Darcy disappear, then looked back at Ruth Ann Blakely, standing above him on the steps. The rain had stopped during lunch and she'd taken off her olive-green raincoat, revealing jeans and a long-sleeved blue T-shirt. Though less snug than her breeches, those jeans left him in no doubt about the feminine curves underneath. Without makeup, and with her hair pulled back in the apparently habitual ponytail, she should have been, well, ordinary. Few women, in Jonah's experience, appeared at their best without cosmetic assistance of one kind or another.

But the trainer's face looked fresh and natural, as if she'd washed it in the morning's rain. Her pink cheeks evidently owed their color to fresh air and plenty of exercise. She had to be strong, judging by the way she'd carried Darcy's suitcases as if they weighed nothing at all. He couldn't be sure about her eye color, which might be hazel or green, but that zestful spark was unmistakable. There was an air of energy about Ms. Blakely, a vibrancy he'd rarely encountered.

"You can leave now," she told him. "You're free."

She also had to be one of the rudest women he'd ever met. "I'd planned to help Darcy unpack," he said, keeping his tone level. "Is that possible?"

"Nope." She shook her head, and the ponytail bounced. "Darcy will manage just fine. It's her stuff, after all. I've got to ask—how did you get all of that in your tiny little Porsche? Did you tie the suitcases on top?"

"I drive a truck when necessary," Jonah told her, feeling his patience start to shred.

"You mean an SUV, right? One of the big, gas-guzzling fancy models with leather seats and Surround Sound and individual heating vents?"

"No. I mean a six-year old diesel pickup with a dented right rear side panel where I hit a fence post." He stopped to think a second. "It does have leather seats."

Arms crossed over her chest, she nodded. "Of course."

"So could I stay around and take the suitcases away when

Darcy's finished with them?" He hated leaving her alone in this place where she knew no one.

Ms. Blakely descended to stand beside him. "Each floor of the dormitory has a box room where the girls store their luggage. Darcy will put all her bags—and whatever's in them that doesn't fit into her room—there." She gripped his upper arm with one strong hand and gazed into his face. "Really, you can leave. We'll take care of her."

Hazel. Ruth Ann Blakely's irises were a mosaic of green and gold flecks, Jonah realized, framed by thick brown lashes. He read empathy in those jade-and-topaz eyes, maybe even compassion. He was surprisingly tempted to accept her understanding, to trust the reassurance she offered.

Fortunately, he came to his senses in the next moment. "Thanks. I'm sure you will." Pulling out of her grasp, he ran down the remaining steps and only then stopped to look back. "By the way, we have a meeting tomorrow morning at nine. I'd appreciate your timely arrival. My schedule is rather tight. Since your input is vital to the project, I'd like to get started as early as possible."

He walked away without waiting for her to respond.

And he pretended not to hear when she said, "Oh, yes, sir, of course, sir, Mr. Architectural Pain in the Rear! Sir!"

Chapter Three

Ruth Ann entered the Hawkridge Manor library at twenty minutes after eight the next morning. She settled herself at the far end of the table from the easel set up for Jonah Granger's use and set about finishing her cinnamon roll and coffee while she waited.

At eight forty-five, Granger strode into the room. Without glancing in Ruth Ann's direction, he extracted his work from a carrying case and placed the sheets on the easel. Flipping through them, he changed the order a couple of times.

Ruth Ann grinned to herself. The great man seemed a little nervous about his presentation.

What he didn't have to be nervous about was his appearance. Today's V-necked sweater in a heathery green wool, worn over a T-shirt and dark jeans, looked every bit as good as last week's dressier outfit. The man was incapable of showing up unprepared, unlike Ruth Ann, who had to make a special effort to leave the barn without wearing pieces of hay and smears of horse feed.

She would give him the style points, but she claimed a victory when it came to patience. Twice, he looked at the clock on the wall and verified the time there with his watch, then glanced at the doorway and shook his head. Ruth Ann didn't doubt he was waiting for her to show up.

The third time he checked the clock, she decided to grant his wish. She cleared her throat loudly, taking great pleasure in his jump of surprise.

"What the—?" He jerked around and saw her sitting at the end of the table, relaxed and grinning. His brows lowered in a frown, almost meeting on the bridge of that arrogant, aquiline nose. "How long have you been there?"

"Long enough. You just knew I'd be late, didn't you?"

"I'm surprised that you aren't." He fingered through the drawings once more—regaining control, Ruth Ann thought. "I checked in with Jayne on the way up. She'll be here as soon as nine o'clock classes start."

"Exactly what is this meeting about, anyway?"

Paging through a notebook, Granger didn't spare her so much as a glance. "You."

The answer caught her unawares. Ruth Ann sat up straight in her chair, letting her boot heels thunk on the floor. "What about me?"

He snapped the notebook closed, put it down, then stepped over to prop one hip on the corner of the table.

"You're the one with the major objections to the project. You're the one who would be working in the building I design. Therefore, you are the person who has to be convinced that my ideas for the new stable at Hawkridge are feasible." The grin he sent her had a malicious edge to it. "Don't you like being the center of attention?"

"No." She had lost the upper hand somehow. On her feet, Ruth Ann headed for the door, needing light and air, a chance to think....

Jonah Granger stood at the same moment and moved to

block her path. Her momentum brought her right up against him, with her chest pressed into his ribs. His hands closed over her shoulders, vetoing any move to escape.

"You're going to run away instead?" He lifted one eyebrow, giving his face a sardonic expression. "You don't have the guts to face the situation and really decide which of us is right?"

Ruth Ann glared up at him, speechless with too many emotions to name—foremost among them being fury that he read her too easily, along with a weird sort of shiver as her body touched his. "I—You—"

"Here we are." Jayne Thomas entered carrying a tray with a coffeepot and cups. Miriam Edwards followed, bearing a basket of pastries and bagels.

Suddenly free, Ruth Ann took a long step back at the same time as Jonah pivoted to face the new arrivals. "Good morning, Miriam," he said smoothly. "It's a pleasure to see you again."

Miriam gushed over him, paying Ruth Ann no attention whatsoever. And Ruth Ann was grateful, for once, because she could feel her face flaming red, the way it did whenever she was embarrassed. While the others poured coffee and debated over calories, she walked back to her chair at the end of the table, rubbing her hands over her shoulders to erase the tingles lingering there. Picking up her favorite mug—the one with a cartoon of the front end of a cute pony on one side and the tail end on the other—she took a deep breath, then turned to confront the situation.

"Okay," she said, glad that her voice didn't shake. "I can't spend all morning in here—I've got work to do at the barn. What are we supposed to accomplish?"

She heard Jayne sigh at her bluntness, but Miriam was the one who spoke. "Now, Ruth Ann, dear, I know how attached you are to the old stable, and for good reasons—certainly your family has a history there and we understand that means a lot to you."

Miriam was a well-preserved sixty years old, a lawyer's wife who advertised his success with cashmere sweaters, triple strands of real pearls at her throat and diamonds set in platinum on her fingers. Her coppery hair gleamed in the light from the library's overhead lamps and swung smoothly around her face as she nodded. She kept a string of hunters and polo ponies in her own stable, and wanted the barn at Hawkridge named in her honor.

"I've been thinking since our meeting last week," she continued, including Jonah in her glance, "and it occurred to me that perhaps we don't have to raze the old building. Once we've built the new equestrian facility, we could get the old one cleaned up and use it for...some other purpose."

Before Ruth Ann could object, Jayne leaned forward in her chair. "Come and sit at this end of the table, Ruth Ann. You'll be able to see better. And I can pour you some fresh coffee. I know you live on the stuff."

Reluctantly, Ruth Ann sat down beside Jayne, with Miriam across the table and Granger sitting closest to the easel. A glance at his superior smile set her teeth on edge. Once Jayne handed back her mug, Ruth Ann made sure that the back end of the pony faced Jonah as she took a long sip.

His eyes narrowed as he took in her message. In the next instant, though, the frown smoothed away as he got to his feet. "Miriam, I think that's a good idea, though we're not quite to the stage yet where Ms. Blakely has agreed to cooperate. I thought I would go through my elevations and floor plans again, Ms. Blakely—"

"Oh, for heaven's sake," she interrupted. "Call me Ruth Ann. It's hard to argue effectively using last names."

His grin, now filled with real amusement, surprised her. "True. I'm Jonah. As I was saying, I thought this would give you a chance to voice any thoughts, ask any questions that occur to you."

For Jayne's sake, Ruth Ann bit back the sarcastic comment on the tip of her tongue. "Go ahead," she told Jonah. "Impress me."

The exterior drawings were beautiful renderings of an imposing structure fit for a king, not merely the king's horses. Ruth Ann looked at the headmistress. "Our girls should have such nice quarters. Why don't we make this the new residence hall, instead of a stable?"

Jayne frowned at her. Miriam said, "My sister's new barn blends with its environment and looks like it's always been there. I expect Jonah can do the same with this building, by the time construction and landscaping are complete."

"My stable blends with its environment," Ruth Ann countered, "because it's been there for more than a hundred years. Howard Ridgely used the same brick and stone and timber for the house and the barn. You'll never get new materials to match."

"You'd be surprised what can be achieved with the right tools." Jonah shifted the pages to display an interior view. "A new building can be aged to complement its surroundings." He held up a hand when Ruth Ann started to say something. "Without the kind of deterioration that natural aging inevitably brings about. You get a stronger building with a similar appearance."

And so it went. For every objection Ruth Ann raised, Miriam and Jonah had an explanation of how their stable would be superior. High ceilings, expensive materials, too much space or not enough…nothing she could say broke through their certainty. Jayne appeared to be listening to both sides, but Ruth Ann couldn't tell what conclusions she drew. Anyway, she was only the headmistress—the Board of Directors would tell her what they wanted done and she would execute their orders.

"It's okay, I guess," Ruth Ann said, once Jonah had finished his presentation. "I mean, I'm sure some people would feel privileged to have a barn like this for their horses. But it's too big, for one thing—the number of extra steps you would add to my day would become miles before long. The tack room down there," she said, pointing to the room plan, "and the stalls over here—you've got me carrying saddles and bridles and blankets from one end of the place to the other."

"These details can be modified," Jonah replied in a stiff voice.

"There's no room for hay storage without using stall space. The feed room is on an interior wall, meaning I'll have to bring bags through the aisle rather than being able to use an outside door.

"As for upkeep—have you seen the cobwebs a barn ceiling can accumulate? How am I going to clean those clerestory windows thirty feet off the floor? Horseshoes chip brick floors. Horses chew wood and kick walls—how are you going to feel when your mahogany stall paneling gets smashed? The amount of money needed to keep a place like this in good shape and the number of people required for maintenance are way beyond what the school has been willing or able to fund in the past. I can't—"

"Enough." Jonah held up a hand. "Clearly, this plan doesn't meet with your approval." He looked at Miriam. "I can make changes, of course, to bring the project more in line with Ms. Bla—Ruth Ann's ideas."

Miriam folded her hands together on the table, where her rings twinkled under the lights. "Well, to be frank, Jonah, Ruth

Ann doesn't have final approval for the stable plans. We've solicited her advice, of course, because she's good at her job. But in the end, the board will decide what's to be done about the equestrian facility." Her gaze conveyed no warmth as she glanced in Ruth Ann's direction. "With or without her."

Ruth Ann hadn't expected anything else, though she hadn't thought to hear the truth expressed quite so blatantly this morning. After a couple of seconds, she cleared her throat and nodded. "I understand the situation, Mrs. Edwards. I've already explained my position to Ms. Thomas. I like working at Hawkridge. I think my horses are good for the girls. My stipulation for staying is that we use the old barn—a building constructed by men who knew and loved horses, managed for a century by men who felt the same. My barn has flaws, I grant you, but nothing a careful renovation couldn't correct. I believe the history of the old stable makes it as valuable as the Manor itself to Hawkridge School."

She shrugged. "If the board doesn't see it that way, I'll find another job."

Standing, she moved toward the library exit, careful not to touch Jonah as she passed him. On the threshold, she turned. "I don't know if you're aware of this, but the terms of Howard Ridgely's will, as well as my grandfather's and father's wills, are quite clear. The stable does, as you say, belong to the estate and the school.

"But the horses are mine. If I leave, so do they."

Miriam's gasp was the last thing she heard before she left the room.

IN THE AFTERNOONS of this first week of class, new girls were taken around in small groups to meet the staff members in charge of extracurricular activities. Cultural pursuits—music and various art disciplines—as well as individual and team sports were available, and girls were encouraged to participate in whichever pastimes drew their interest.

Darcy's group visited the stable on Thursday afternoon. She and seven other girls, including Eve, arrived with their upper-class guide, Ingrid, at three-thirty.

"Right on time," Ruth Ann said as she greeted them. "Which is what you should be if you decide to come for lessons or unstructured rides. It's not fair to me or to the horses to leave us standing around waiting for you."

She led them into the stable. "Our horses spend about half the day inside and half out. I bring the darker horses inside during the day, to keep their coats from bleaching in the sunshine. They eat breakfast and dinner inside, then spend the night grazing in the field. Not one of them would bite you out of meanness, but if you hold one finger out, they might think it's a carrot and reach for the treat." Her pantomime of a horse biting off the tip of a finger made the all the girls giggle. Well, all except Eve.

"So keep your fingers together. If you want to pet a horse, you can use the backs of your knuckles softly on their cheeks." She demonstrated on the girl nearest her, provoking smiles. "Feel free to visit up and down the aisle, say hello to any horse that strikes your fancy. Their names are on the stalls."

Most of the girls dispersed along the length of the barn, and soon the horses began poking their heads over the locked bottom halves of their doors, hoping for treats but settling for attention if that was all they could get.

Eve, however, went to the barn entrance and stood looking out, away from the animals.

Ruth Ann went to join her. "You're not into horses?"

The girl shook her head. "They smell. This place smells." She sniffed, then coughed. "Gross."

"I'm willing to concede that the smell of horses and barns isn't appealing to everybody. What do you like to do instead? Tennis? Softball?"

Eve rolled her eyes. "Gag me. Who wants to hit a stupid ball around? And the clothes? Yuck. I run. Alone."

"That's a great workout for your heart and lungs. Do you do any strength training? Keeps your bones healthy, you know." The girl needed some muscle, as well. Her wrists weren't much bigger than broomsticks.

Her response, however, was an impatient sigh. "How much longer do I have to be here?"

Too long, as far as I'm concerned, Ruth Ann answered silently. "Until the rest of the girls are ready to leave. If you'd like to sit in the tack room, there are a few magazines on the table. Maybe even one or two that aren't about horses."

She showed Eve to the tack room, ignored her sniff of derision when she saw the worn sofa and scarred coffee table, then went back to the horses. The girls had evidently picked their favorites and Ingrid, one of her longtime riding students, had been to the feed room for carrots and was supervising the careful delivery of treats.

Darcy, however, had not homed in on a particular animal. She stood in the center of the passage instead, carefully studying each horse, but making no move to get close enough to touch.

"Can't make up your mind?" Ruth Ann asked.

The girl shook her head. "I like white horses."

"Grays, you mean?" When Darcy nodded, Ruth Ann said, "Come with me."

She led the way outside, across the cobble-stone stable yard with its curving brick walls, and out to the pasture.

"These are our grays," she told Darcy. "Maybe one of these would be your favorite."

A drawn-out "Oooh" was Darcy's comment as she folded her arms on the top board of the fence and propped her chin on her hands. "They're so beautiful!!"

Ruth Ann had to agree—the grays were her pride and joy. The eight of them looked over, ears pricked, as she and Darcy approached, no doubt wondering if dinnertime had come earlier than usual today. Gradually, the animals went back to grazing the fall grass, creating a portrait of peace in their pale-green pasture against a backdrop of dark evergreen and gold-tinged hardwood trees, with the blue-green Smoky Mountains in the distance.

"Tell me about them," Darcy commanded. "What are their names?"

A glance over her shoulder told Ruth Ann that the rest of the girls—minus Eve—were coming to join them. After more exclamations, she included them all in her introductions.

"Waldo is the largest of all the horses we have here, and the oldest, at twenty-three. He's a Percheron gelding." She spelled the breed name for them. "Percherons were developed to do heavy work, like plowing or pulling carriages. They're very much like the horses knights would have ridden into battle in the olden days, wearing armor and carrying shields and swords." In answer to a question, she said, "Gelding means that his testicles were removed so he can't mate with the mares. That happened to him a long time ago."

After the giggles died down, she introduced the mares— Sheba and Gizelle, both Arabians, petite and fast, the lovely dappled gray Dutch warmblood, Silver Filigree, and the thoroughbred sisters Crystal, Diamond and Lainey, short for Porcelaine.

"Are they triplets?" one of the girls asked.

Ruth Ann shook her head. "Horses usually only have one baby at a time. Lainey's ten years old, then Diamond is nine and Crystal eight. All three are really good jumpers."

"What's the tiny pony's name?" Darcy asked. "Do you ride her?"

"That's Snowflake." Ruth Ann led the girls along the fence, closer to the pony in question, only about forty inches tall. "She's a miniature horse—this is as big as she'll ever get, and she's already thirteen years old. We have a cart she can pull, but we don't have anyone small enough to sit in it right now, so she has a good time just hanging out in the pasture."

Snowflake ambled up to the fence and gave everyone a chance to stroke her nose and sides. Then Ruth Ann herded the girls back to the barn and into the tack room with Eve, where she explained about taking lessons and the types of riding they could learn.

"You'll get a form to fill out on Friday," she told them, "where you can list the sports and other activities you'd like to try, in the order you're most interested. If riding is your number-one favorite, you should put it at the top. Next week I'll be setting up lesson schedules and we'll get started. Any questions?"

Eve raised her hand. "Can we leave now?"

Fortunately, several other girls had legitimate questions, so Darcy's roommate would have to wait. Finally, though, Ingrid headed them toward the Manor and the dorms. Darcy hung back as everyone left.

"Did you have a question?" Ruth Ann collected the magazines Eve had left scattered over the table and on the floor.

"C-could I…" Darcy shook her head. "Never mind." She got out the door before Ruth Ann managed to catch her hand and stop her.

"What did you want? Darcy, look at me." Finally, she had to turn the girl's face toward her to see her dark-brown eyes. "Ask your question. It's okay."

"I just wondered if…if I could watch you feed the horses."

As Ruth Ann stared, the words came tumbling out. "I'll stay out of your way I won't touch them or anything, I promise. I won't make them mad or hurt them. I just want to watch."

"Whoa." Ruth Ann took one of Darcy's hands in both of her own. "Slow down. Relax." She saw that Ingrid was holding up the rest of the group, waiting for Darcy. "She's staying here," Ruth Ann called. "I'll bring her to dinner myself."

Ingrid nodded, waved, and turned away, with the girls following. Still holding Darcy's hand, Ruth Ann went back into the tack room. "Sit down for a second."

Looking scared to death, Darcy dropped onto the couch. She had a habit of keeping her arms folded around her waist, for protection or camouflage, Ruth Ann wasn't sure which.

Moving the magazines, Ruth Ann sat on the coffee table directly across from Darcy. "You're welcome to stay and watch," she said. "I need to see how you are around the horses, to be sure that you're safe. Jonah said you'd broken your arm earlier this year?"

Darcy nodded. "In May, at a horse show. Rufus jumped a crossbar fence and I fell off. Before they caught him, he ran through a couple of other fences, tripped, and strained his leg. It was gonna take him months to get better."

"That's too bad for Rufus. I guess your broken arm needed a few months to heal, too, didn't it?"

The girl shrugged. "It was okay. I don't like swimming, anyway, so I stayed in the house."

"Maybe Rufus doesn't like jumping in the summer heat, either."

"Oh, no." Darcy looked shocked at the idea. "He loves to jump. My mother was going to take him to Europe with her, until he got hurt. He would have competed with some of the best three-year-olds in Germany."

"You were jumping on a three-year-old? Have you done that much riding, Darcy?"

"Since I was five." She sighed and shook her head. "But I don't seem to get better at it."

"What's Rufus like?" Ruth Ann asked the question, though she thought she could predict the answer.

"He's a seventeen-hand chestnut thoroughbred with a white blaze and four white socks," the girl recited, as if she were reading off a sale list. "Really eager, jumps four feet and over, no problem."

"Well, I don't know about you, but I'd be scared to death sitting on a young horse that big." Ruth Ann stood up and motioned for Darcy to do the same. "Sounds like a recipe for disaster. I'd give him another two or three years before I'd trust him not to dump me at a fence."

"Oh, he didn't dump me. I just…fell. I'm too fa— clumsy to ride."

"Right." Ruth Ann relaxed her jaw and tried not to hate Jonah Granger and his wife. "Okay, the way this works is, I clean up a stall, then walk the horse out to the pasture and bring one in. It's kind of labor-intensive, but since I'm the one doing the work, nobody complains. All these horses are calm—no Rufuses here to worry about. So you just stand there and talk to them while I muck out. Okay?"

Darcy nodded. "Okay."

Four horses later, as they walked back in from the pasture with Filigree, Ruth Ann asked casually if Darcy wanted to hold the lead rope. "Fili is a very sensible lady," she promised.

"She knows how to walk quietly beside you without making a fuss."

"O-okay." Darcy took the rope and held it correctly, about a foot from Fili's chin with one hand, gathering the rest in her other hand. As Ruth Ann dropped back slightly, the girl and the mare walked without incident to the waiting stall. Darcy was so busy talking to the horse that she didn't even think about leading Fili into the stall, where she turned her around, unbuckled the halter and stepped back outside to shut the door.

"Very good," Ruth Ann told her. "Seeing you handle Fili, I can believe you've been around horses since you were little. You're good with them, Darcy, calm and sure of yourself."

The girl blushed bright pink, and she didn't say anything. But her eyes shone with happiness.

Once they'd led the grays in, Ruth Ann set the manure fork aside. "I'll clean up the last four stalls after dinner. We can just take these guys out to the pasture, and then I'll walk you back to the Manor."

The glow in Darcy's face faded. "Okay."

Leaving the indoor horses with hay to munch on, Ruth Ann showed Darcy the path from the stable back to the Manor. "You're welcome to come visit any time. You don't have to ride if you don't want to. Horses are fun just to talk to or look at. As Winston Churchill said, 'The outside of a horse is good for the inside of a man.' Or woman."

"Maybe I will," Darcy said. But she didn't sound very certain. "I have to get my homework done, too. And practice my music."

"That's true, though I always thought there was time enough for horses and homework. I never got to do music."

"Did you go to Hawkridge?"

"No, I went to the public schools out in town. But my dad

managed the stable, so I was here every afternoon and all weekend, working with him."

"Was it fun?"

"Well, sure. I loved being with the horses."

"Did you like working with your dad?"

Now there was a tough question. "He could be picky, sometimes, and he'd get mad if I didn't do something just the way he wanted it. But he was a great trainer and taught me all I know about horses."

Once they reached the manicured lawns surrounding the Manor, they could see other girls heading toward the dormitory to prepare for dinner. Ruth Ann glanced at the jeans and sneakers and sweatshirt Darcy had worn to the barn.

"Guess you'd better get changed in a hurry." She checked her watch. "You've got ten minutes before the warning chime."

"Okay." That seemed to be Darcy's favorite word. As she veered away, though, she stopped and looked back at Ruth Ann. "I had fun this afternoon. Thank you."

"You're welcome, Darcy. Like I said, come back anytime."

Ruth Ann watched the girl walk with dragging steps toward the residence hall. In the two hours they'd spent together, she'd gained the impression that Darcy's energy level was dialed to Low—she simply didn't put out much effort, even with the horses. She seemed competent with the animals, but uncertain of herself, reminding Ruth Ann of a child outside the toy store, nose pressed against the window as she stared at the gifts she knew she couldn't buy, wouldn't receive.

Jayne Thomas would be able to provide an explanation for Darcy's behavior. Maybe a conference with the counselor and Darcy's teachers would be a good idea. Ruth Ann wanted to know what she would be dealing with as she worked with Darcy, what sore points to avoid and what counseling techniques to use.

She was so deep in thought she hadn't noticed anyone approaching. When a hand closed around her elbow, she gasped and automatically assumed a defensive posture.

Jonah Granger gave a derisive snort. "Going to take me out with a kick and a karate chop?"

Ruth Ann jerked her arm free. "Why are you sneaking up on me? What are you doing here? Parents aren't allowed to visit until Thanksgiving."

"But architects are," he countered. "So I came looking for you."

Chapter Four

"Looking for me? Why?"

Before Jonah could answer, a bell rang inside the building.

"Dinner," Ruth Ann explained, at his questioning look. "What do you want?"

He gave a brief laugh. "For dinner?"

She didn't get the joke. "What—do—you—want—" she said slowly, emphasizing syllables and consonants, "—that compels you to come searching for me on Thursday evening at dinnertime?"

A glance at the Manor showed Jonah the brightly lit dining-hall windows. Inside, girls were congregating at tables as the staff set out food. Some of the teachers he'd met were present, as well. "Are you supposed to be in there?" He nodded in the direction he'd been staring.

Ruth Ann shrugged one shoulder. "I usually have dinner in the hall, so I don't have to cook. But I'm not assigned to a particular table this year."

"In other words, you don't have to check in for the meal?"

"No." She folded her arms over her chest. "What are you getting at?"

"Why don't we go into town and get something to eat? Then I can explain why I'm here."

The only part of Ruth Ann that moved in response to his question was her jaw, which dropped and left her mouth hanging open.

When she didn't say anything, Jonah nodded. "I'll take that as a yes. Come on." He grabbed her wrist and turned toward the Porsche, parked in the circular drive.

But Ruth Ann—of course—pulled free. "I won't go three yards with you, let alone to dinner."

Hearing the venom in her tone, he swung back around. "What are you so mad about?"

"I just spent a couple of hours with your stepdaughter. And the only thing I'm left to wonder is how she managed to become such a likeable girl, given the way she's been treated." She lifted her chin and actually looked down her nose at him, as if he were a slimy creature just come out from under a rock. "With parents like you, the poor girl certainly doesn't need any enemies."

Pivoting on her heel, she started to walk away. But Jonah caught up, grabbed her wrist again and pulled her back around. "What the hell are you talking about?"

Ruth Ann glanced down at his hand, then back into his face. "Let go of me."

Jonah gave her arm a sharp shake. "Not until you tell me what I need to know. What did Darcy say?"

She ignored the question. "I'm telling you again—let go. Or you will be sorry."

"If you'd just—" He saw the spark in her eyes, realized she was about to explode and released her arm. "Okay, okay." He raised his hands and backed up several steps. "Look, I don't care what you think you know—I've never hurt Darcy in my life and I don't believe she told you anything different."

"Darcy said she was put on a horse she was scared of, a horse far too big and green for any but the most experienced adult rider. She fell off at a jump and got blamed because the horse—a poorly trained and badly managed animal, I'm sure—hurt itself. And then she was told she fell because she was clumsy and fat. How cruel could you be?"

Jonah dropped his chin to his chest. "Brittany—her mother, my *ex*-wife—that's who the poison came from." Shaking his head, he scrubbed a hand over his face. "I wasn't there, though I'd be glad if Darcy never went near a horse again, since broken bones and an overdose of pain medicine is all she's achieved with the beasts so far."

When he looked up, Ruth Ann was staring at him with a shocked expression. "Darcy took too much medicine?"

He nodded. "We had to have her stomach pumped. That's why she's here. At Hawkridge."

The cool darkness fell around them as they gazed at each other across ten feet of grass. Finally, Ruth Ann stirred. "Maybe we do need to talk. I have to know more."

"Let's go." This time, he simply motioned her to walk toward the car ahead of him. The lady was dangerous to the touch.

But she didn't move, and he heard her deep intake of breath. "I can't go anywhere in these clothes. I'd have to change. And some of the horses haven't been fed. I can't leave until my work is finished. So, really, it's just a bad idea. Maybe we could meet tomorrow morning—"

Jonah shook his head. "We tried that today." Now that he'd come up with the idea of dinner with Ruth Ann, he couldn't face going back to town to eat dinner alone in his hotel room. "How long will it take you to feed the horses and change?"

"An hour, at least. Too long for you to wait."

He glanced at his watch. "It's barely six o'clock. Most people in Manhattan don't eat until nine."

"This isn't Manhattan."

"Thank God. So here's what we'll do—go back and feed your animals, then meet me in Ridgeville. What kind of food do you want? Not that we have many options—there's the pizza place, the café, the diner or the steakhouse. I've eaten in all four this week already. Take your pick."

Ruth Ann made a helpless gesture. "I—I don't know."

"Okay, I'll choose. The café has a more varied menu, so I'll see you there in an hour." When he reached the Porsche, he glanced back, just to be sure she'd started toward the stable.

But, no, she was still standing where he'd left her. "Ruth Ann!" Jonah yelled. "Get moving!"

To his relief, she whirled and disappeared into the dark.

He sank into the seat of the Porsche, not bothering to stifle the groan this time, and put the key in the ignition. Before he could start the engine, though, his cell phone beeped, indicating a missed call. He flipped the top open and noted the number with a curse.

"The last person on the planet I want to talk to," he muttered, turning the car key. "I don't need your particular brand of harassment right now, Brittany."

Nevertheless, once he'd reached the café parking lot and set the emergency brake, he returned his ex-wife's call.

"It's about time you got back to me," she said, in place of hello. "I called an hour ago."

"What do you want, Brittany?"

"I want to know how Darcy is doing, of course. Is she simply miserable at that school you insisted on sending her to?"

"I didn't think she looked miserable on Monday, which is the last time I saw her."

"You haven't checked on her since Monday?"

"Parent visits tend to upset the girls, I'm told. The counselors suggest staying away until they've had a chance to work with the student and make some progress."

"Are you sure this school is legitimate? Maybe it's just a—a front for child molesters."

Jonah thought of Jayne Thomas's kind eyes, Ruth Ann's blunt honesty. "Darcy is in good hands, Brittany. If that's all—"

"No, don't hang up." She hesitated, which was unusual for Brittany. "I've been thinking about you, Jonah. About us."

Just what he needed. "There is no us. I have legal papers to that effect. And canceled alimony checks."

"But we have a child, Jonah. She draws us together."

He snorted into the phone. "Give me a break. You abandoned your daughter in July when you flitted off to Europe with…what was his name? Jean? Gilles? Jacques? What about *that* draws us together?"

"I know I deserve all of what you're saying, and more. But I'm willing to change. Just give me a chance."

"Listen carefully, Brittany. No way. In fact, there is no way in hell I'd let you back into my life. Don't worry about Darcy and don't bother me again." He cut the connection with a flick of his thumb. Before he could toss it into the passenger seat, it rang again.

He checked the caller ID, and, as soon as he said, "Hi, Stephen," his business partner in Manhattan launched into a tirade about the latest abuses and demands of his own clients, interspersed with accusations concerning Jonah's mistakes relating to the company and its affairs. Though the two of them pursued their design projects separately, Stephen enacted this ritual of complaint and blame several times a week as a way of asserting his control of the firm. Jonah made noises of agreement or disagreement where expected until the storm passed over and hung up. Then he dropped the phone on the passenger seat and left the car.

Trying to shed the tension his business partner had generated, Jonah gave some thought to the phone call from Brittany. His ex-wife must be feeling vulnerable, if she could actually admit she'd been wrong. This last affair hadn't lasted long— only a matter of months. Then again, she wasn't as young or as talented a rider as some of the women she competed against in Europe. Jean–Gilles–Jacques had probably found himself an adoring twenty-something to train horses for. Brittany, to her dismay, would turn forty in less than six weeks. Jonah hated admitting that he, too, had been one of her younger men.

Between the two of them, his business partner and his ex-wife had managed to put a major dent in his mood. With half of the hour he'd given Ruth Ann left to wait, Jonah went into the café and ordered the best Scotch the bar offered, on the rocks. Then he sat staring into the glass, jiggling the amber liquid back and forth over the cubes as he wondered if Darcy really was all right. Five nights alone, in a place she hated, would be torture....

"I'm here."

He jerked his head up at the breathless announcement to find Ruth Ann standing beside him. For a minute, looking up at her, Jonah was breathless, too.

She'd taken out the ponytail, and her hair fell softly around her face. sun-streaked gold over a glossy brown the shade of oak leaves in November. Her cheeks were pinker than usual, her lashes darker, her lips—full and pouty, he noticed for the first time—redder. She'd put on a little makeup. For him?

And good clothes. A soft green turtleneck shaped the fullness of her breasts. Dark-brown corduroy slacks molded the generous curves of her hips, the firm muscles of her thighs....

That was far enough. As he got to his feet, Jonah slapped his brain back onto the sanity track. "You *are* here." He glanced at his watch. "And only ten minutes late. Are you sure all the horses got fed?"

Ruth Ann nodded. "They did. I have to throw out more hay when I get back, but that's easy enough."

"Then sit down and rest for awhile. Let me order you a drink." He raised a hand to get the waiter's attention. "It's hard work, taking care of horses. Especially so many, and by yourself. You don't have any help at all?"

The waiter wandered over and she asked for a duplicate of Jonah's drink, then said, "I do have a farmer who deals with cleaning up the fields. He uses the manure as fertilizer on his crops. Horses make about fifty pounds a day, you know. That's more than three tons a week, from my herd alone."

Jonah winced. "Appetizing thought."

She smiled, her eyes crinkling at the corners. "A few of the girls help me out in the afternoons. And sometimes students who need an attitude adjustment are sent to work with me in the stable. A week of mucking stalls usually convinces them that making trouble isn't…ahem…worth the consequences."

Her drink arrived. She took a sip, let the whiskey sit on her tongue for a moment, then swallowed, with an "mmmmm."

"You're a connoisseur?" Jonah asked.

Ruth Ann shook her head. "My dad and granddad were the connoisseurs. They could detect a dozen different labels by taste without seeing the bottles. I know when I've got a good one, but I don't do much drinking."

"Ah." He thought about proposing a toast, then dropped the idea. This wasn't a social occasion. He'd wanted to talk with her about the project. And she wanted to know about Darcy.

His next question came out before he'd thought about it. "Is

Darcy okay?" Then he did think about it. "I mean, she's not used to boarding school. Is she settling in, feeling comfortable?"

He wanted an immediate "Yes." Unfortunately for his peace of mind, Ruth Ann looked down into her glass and didn't answer right away.

"I think so," she said finally. "I've caught glimpses of her at meals, sitting with a couple of girls and, it seemed, joining in the conversation. Usually, roommates tend to hang around together. But Eve…" She shrugged. "I don't think Eve and Darcy have exactly bonded."

"That would be like a piranha bonding with a kitten." When Ruth Ann gave him a reproving look, he shrugged. "Well, she's just like her mother, and her mother chews nails for breakfast."

"So you know her from New York?"

"No, but I know her type."

The hostess came to tell them their table was ready. As Ruth Ann stood up, she said, "Generalizations aren't necessarily accurate. Or kind."

Jonah waited until she was seated before sitting down. "She tried to sell me real estate within an hour of meeting."

"But in a man, you'd find that admirable, call it aggressive marketing. A woman who behaves the same way gets castigated as a piranha, implying she's a killer."

He chuckled. "Are you a feminist, by any chance?"

"I'm a human being. I'd like to see us all treated equally." She took another sip of Scotch, then leaned forward and folded her arms on the table. "Going back to your question— I think Darcy's doing okay, for the end of the first week. Believe me, every teacher, every staff member, has their eyes peeled, keeping track of the new girls. The counselor makes time for each new student during these first days, twice, if at all possible. We know it's a tough transition. We keep them busy and try not to give them too much time to think about home, their friends, the life they left."

The tension inside his chest uncoiled, and Jonah leaned back in his chair, finally able to relax. "Thanks. I needed to hear that."

"But now I need the answers to my questions." Ruth Ann took her arms off the table and picked up the menu. "Darcy is at Hawkridge, I gather, because she's depressed and attempted suicide." Over the top of the leather folder, her hazel gaze caught and held his own. "I want to know why."

He started to answer, but the waiter arrived to take their order, went for wine and returned almost right away. Just as Jonah approved the bottle, their appetizers were brought to the table. All in all, more than ten minutes passed before they had the table to themselves again.

"Are you going to help me out or not?" Ruth Ann said, frowning at him over her cream of mushroom soup.

"Yes, ma'am!" Jonah shot back at her. "When we've got some privacy. It's not my fault everything came at once."

Still, he took a sip of chardonnay *and* a bite of his spanakopita before he spoke. "When I met Darcy, she was a first-grader, a sweet little girl with a round face and bouncy brown curls."

"You were dating her mother, I take it?"

Jonah nodded. "Her father—Brittany's second husband, who was in his sixties—died when Darcy was four. I didn't see much of her—she seemed to spend a lot of time with her grandparents, Brittany's mother and father, or at a friend's house."

Ruth Ann snorted into her wineglass. "That was what Brittany wanted you to believe, anyway."

He conceded the point with a tilt of his head. "Could be. I didn't know much about children, but I was glad to agree when Brittany suggested I adopt Darcy. I assumed I'd have time to get to know her once we were living in the same house. Somehow, though, it didn't happen that way."

"Maybe you just didn't try hard enough."

He frowned as he looked at her. "I was fresh out of design school when I met Brittany. I've spent the last seven years establishing my business and my reputation—that means working twenty hours a day, sometimes, five, six, even seven days a week. I spent time with Darcy whenever I had it to spare."

She swallowed hard. "Sorry."

He was quiet while the server removed their appetizer dishes and replaced them with the steaks they'd both ordered. "Brittany has always owned horses," he said when they were alone again. "She's won championships in jumping competitions all over the world. Darcy was supposed to follow in her footsteps."

Mashing butter into her baked potato, Ruth Ann nodded. "She definitely loves them. She wanted to watch me feed them this evening."

"I know she does. And when I visited the stable with Brittany, I thought Darcy enjoyed riding the small horses and ponies. After her ninth birthday, though, Brittany moved Darcy onto bigger mounts, started making her jump fences. They'd return from riding lessons, arguing as they walked in the door about mistakes Darcy had made with this horse or that. She went through a growth spurt when she was about ten or eleven—she shot up five inches in one year and gained about thirty pounds. Brittany was simply horrified."

Ruth Ann raised a hand to stop him. "Let me guess. Brittany is five-seven, one hundred ten pounds, wears a size two and has the same shiny brown hair as her daughter, worn short but always perfectly neat."

"You've met, have you?"

She rolled her eyes. "I know the type."

His grin made her heart flutter. "She had long hair when we got married. Anyway, after that, Darcy was constantly on diets, eating salads for dinner, plain tuna sandwiches for lunch, no desserts or snacks. The housekeeper told me once that it made her cry to fix that kind of meal for Darcy to take to school."

After staring at his half-eaten steak for a few seconds, he pushed it to the side. "Anyway, that's the way it's been the last two years. I realized fast enough that Brittany was a major mistake in my life. Our divorce was final a year ago. We have joint custody, and I've tried to see Darcy at least every other week, if only for a couple of hours, but Brittany's still good at keeping her out of sight. I didn't know about the broken arm incident until Darcy herself called me from the hospital after Brittany had left for the night to go out on a date."

"Poor baby." Looking down at her own meal, Ruth Ann swallowed the lump in her throat. "I don't seem to be hungry anymore."

"Then Brittany called me in July when she found Darcy passed out on the couch with an empty bottle of pain pills in her hand. As we waited in the emergency room, Brittany told me she was headed to Europe for a jumping tour, leaving Darcy at the house in New York. She asked if I would check on her occasionally."

Ruth Ann allowed the disgust on her face to be her only comment.

Jonah nodded. "That was the point when I decided I had to get Darcy away from her mother. I brought her to live with me while she recuperated from the broken arm. I'd already been retained to work on the Hawkridge project, and when I looked into the school, I realized this might be my answer."

"Brittany just let you enroll her daughter without protest?"

"As long as she's not required to disrupt her schedule, I don't think Brittany cares where Darcy goes."

"Nice. Most dogs have better instincts with their young."

"I know. When I realized how Brittany treated her daughter, I knew I wouldn't be having children with her. Then, when I realized she was sleeping with her trainer, well…" He shrugged. "She's an amoral, unpleasant woman with a lot of money. I was too young, too busy, too stupid to see it at first."

The waiter returned with the dessert tray, which they both refused, and offered coffee, which they accepted. Ruth Ann took hers black, but Jonah stirred in cream and three lumps of sugar.

"Where did you meet Brittany?" Ruth Ann wasn't sure he'd answer such a nosy question, but she decided to give it a try. "Why would you be attracted to her in the first place?"

But Jonah didn't seem to mind. "I was overseeing the construction of Mrs. Edwards's sister's barn. Brittany was the interior designer, so our jobs overlapped. I thought we had similar approaches to the work, to life. She's beautiful, sexy as hell, seductive if she wants to be." He shrugged. "I was a horny kid who'd spent his whole life in school. Architects are often misfits among their peers, so they don't necessarily have great social lives. I was…flattered…that this sophisticated older woman wanted me." He grimaced into his coffee cup. "'Pride goeth before a fall.'"

Ruth Ann kept her face blank as she studied Jonah's face. Of course he would be drawn to beautiful women, and they to him. He was the most gorgeous man she'd ever seen. And tonight he'd shown more sensitivity to Darcy's plight than she'd expected. He might even be likeable, for all the good that would do her. Beautiful, sexy as hell, seductive… Not adjectives even her closest friends would use to describe Ruth Ann Blakely.

"Well, at least I know the background now," she told him, stirring in her chair. "I can help Darcy work on her self-image. I doubt she's too clumsy to ride—almost everyone can sit a horse, given the right animal and good instruction. Her weight is distributed more above her hips than below, which makes her top-heavy, but that's not an insurmountable problem." A thought occurred to her. "Do you ride?"

"I stay on, even over the jumps, though not necessarily with finesse. The schools I attended didn't have horses, but my college roommate did, and I picked it up visiting him."

"Maybe you could— Wait." Ruth Ann reconsidered his exact words. "The schools you attended? What does that mean?"

"My parents were out of the country quite often, so I went to boarding schools from the time I was twelve."

"Were they fugitives from justice?" She winked, to show him she was teasing.

His grin reassured her. "Not quite that bad. Research anthropologists, in fact. Their work focuses on some of the indigenous peoples of Central and South America. I've spent more time in the rain forest than I really want to remember."

"I'm not a fan of hot and muggy, myself. What I was about to suggest was that you could do some riding with Darcy at Thanksgiving, and over the winter vacation. As a way of getting closer to her, I mean."

"Maybe. I was wondering, though, if I could watch when… if…she takes lessons." He held up a hand. "I'm aware that's not strictly allowed. But I'd like to know she's doing okay."

He was hard to resist, when he looked so concerned, so caring. "I'll think about it," Ruth Ann said. Later, when he'd annoyed her again, as he surely would, she'd find the strength to enforce the rules.

His pleased smile made her want to give in right away. "Thanks." He picked up the coffeepot the waiter had left on their table. "More?"

Ruth Ann shook her head and scooted her chair back. "I've got to be going. Hay to throw out, you know."

The pot hit the table with a loud thunk. "You can't leave yet." His voice was mild, his expression pleasant enough, but his tone was urgent. "We haven't even begun to discuss why I came looking for you."

"It's almost ten o'clock, and I'm up at five. I need to get home."

"*We* need to discuss the stable project at Hawkridge." His shoulders stiffened. "Miriam Edwards wants to build a new barn, and she's provided plenty of money to that end. She doesn't want to have to buy new horses, as well. You dropped a bombshell on her the other morning by announcing that the animals belong to you."

"That's exactly what I meant to do. So why don't you design her an auditorium and concert hall? I can see it now— The Miriam Edwards Center for the Performing Arts. Sounds perfect—the school needs one and I won't have a word to say about it."

"I can't persuade her to sponsor a performing arts center because she's every bit as stubborn as you are." He made a visible effort to scale back his temper. "Now, why can't we compromise? I have some ideas—"

"Of course you do." Ruth Ann expended zero effort on remaining calm. "But are they good ideas? You said yourself, you manage to stay on horses, but you don't *know* them. You've never worked in a barn, yet you're trying to design one, without asking for input from the person who will be working there."

"That's what I'm doing now!"

She stood up. "Well, I'm sorry, Jonah, but it's too little, too late. You should have called me when you were first working up the plans."

He got to his feet, as well. "Miriam suggested waiting, said you'd be easier to deal with when we had a complete proposal."

"Your mistake was believing her."

"Right, but I'm trying to correct that mistake. If you'll let me."

"Are you willing to consider renovating my barn, rather than designing a brand-new building?" Jonah hesitated, and Ruth Ann nodded. "Right. You want this project to be all about you. You don't give a damn about my barn, or its value as historical and architectural evidence. You've come up with this wild concept of a stable and now you want to modify it somehow and get me to sign off on the project. That's not going to happen."

Pulling her wallet out of her back pocket, she thumbed out three twenty-dollar bills. "I think this covers my share. Thanks for the drink and for giving me the information I need. 'Bye."

Walking fast, Ruth Ann threaded her way through the tables to the front of the café. Because people sitting beside the windows could see her, she forced herself to walk to her truck, rather than run.

But once on the road, she ignored the speed limit in her haste to escape.

Chapter Five

The trouble with her truck, though, was that it didn't have the speed and steering of a Porsche. Long before she reached the Hawkridge gates, Jonah's headlights came up behind her. At the right moment, he swung out to the left side and swept past, then zoomed back into the lane ahead of her. His brake lights forced her to slow down, and they made the rest of the trip well within the speed limit, stopping only when they'd reached the circular drive in front of Hawkridge Manor.

Ruth Ann decided to stay in her seat for this confrontation. Gripping the steering wheel with both hands, she waited as Jonah's long strides brought him to her driver's window.

She lowered the pane of glass between them. "Yes?"

"You left without hearing what I had to say."

"I'm pretty sure I know what you have to say."

He shook his head. "Are you always this obstinate?"

"Most people would say so."

"And does this method get you what you want? Are you happy with your life?"

"Of course." She was, for the most part. Except on those nights when the sheets were cold and she didn't have anyone beside her to help warm them up. And the rainy afternoons she sat alone on the couch, reading the paper. "What does that have to do with anything?"

"Just wondering." He stepped closer and rested an arm on her windowsill. "My suggestion, if you'd care to consider it, is that I spend some time in your barn. Let me observe you at work, see what your process is, how you use your tools, how the horses use the space you give them. Then I can modify my plan and come up with a design that you might like."

"Doubtful." The response came automatically. She wouldn't for one second allow him to believe she would abandon her barn.

And the prospect of having Jonah Granger hanging around all day while she worked was daunting, to say the least. How could she function with him scrutinizing her every move? If she tried to give a lesson while he was there, she felt certain the girls would be watching him instead of listening to her instructions. All operations at the barn would pretty much grind to a halt.

She opened her mouth to say no, but Jonah spoke first. "If you don't cooperate, you won't be able to say you gave me an opportunity to improve my design. The board members will discount your opinion as prejudiced and make a decision regardless of your preferences. This is your chance to stop me. If I can't produce, after you give me this chance, then I'm not good enough for the job."

The serpent in the Garden of Eden would have sounded like this, whispering all sorts of temptations into Eve's ear, using Jonah's rich, mesmerizing voice. He'd leaned in close, spoke quietly. She could hear him breathing, and the spicy scent of his cologne reached her on the night breeze.

"Okay," Ruth Ann said, just as Eve had. "If that's what you want to do, you're welcome to come observe."

"Thank you." He didn't move back, though the conversation was essentially finished. "I'll be there tomorrow, if that's okay. Early."

"Fine." She turned her head away, trying to gain some room, and a stray strand of her hair snagged the button on the sleeve of his leather jacket. "Oh…"

"Hold still a minute," he said, and brought up his free hand to untangle her.

The process seemed to take a long time. As she stared through the windshield, Jonah's slight tugs on her scalp sent streams of sparks shooting all through her body, leaving her chest hollow and the rest of her shaky.

"There you go," he said, finally. When she looked over, he was staring back at her, his blue eyes gleaming like silver in the dark, the sensuous form of his lips shaped by curves of shadow.

"You're free," he said softly. Then he wiggled his fingers in the space right next to her cheek.

Was it her imagination, or had his fingertips touched her skin? "Um…thanks." She blinked, trying to separate fantasy from reality. "See you…um…in the morning."

With a slap at the door panel, he stepped back. "I'll be there. 'Night."

Jonah walked back to the Porsche without watching Ruth Ann drive away. Sitting inside, though, he didn't start the engine immediately. He flexed his hand, the one with fingertips still tingling from where they'd grazed her soft, cool cheek. On a crazy impulse, he sniffed at the ends of his fingers. No scent of makeup lingered with him. The clean, natural texture of her skin left no trace at all.

And why that turned him on, he couldn't begin to explain.

Muttering a rude word, he started the car and gunned the engine, then took the curved driveway too fast. He'd been celibate a long time. The divorce had left him with a hangover of sorts—a woman-sized headache and a lack of desire to indulge himself again. So his response to Ruth Ann might be the signal that he was ready to play. He'd probably react in a similar way to any female in close proximity.

Not that she was unattractive. Different than his usual style of date, of course. But round in the right places, where those women were not, with a unique and potent appeal in her gold-green eyes and silky hair. He'd always been a sucker for girls with long hair.

Once outside the Hawkridge gates, Jonah pushed the Porsche's speed up and concentrated on his driving, taking the mountain's hairpin curves faster than the law would allow. Speed proved an effective antidote to confusion. By the time he reached his hotel room, the adrenaline rush had subsided, leaving him tired and ready for sleep.

But he woke more than once during the night, each time aware he'd seen horses—big gray horses—racing through his dreams.

RUTH ANN'S eyes popped open at 4:00 a.m. and stayed that way. After fifteen minutes, she gave up trying to go back to sleep and got up to dress for the day. As she drank her coffee and spooned her way through hot oatmeal with raisins and brown sugar, she refused to acknowledge the struggle she'd faced in choosing not to wear a nice sweater, a new pair of breeches and her leather jacket. The surest way to ruin good clothes was to wear them to take care of horses.

In the silence, she could hear rain dripping off the eaves of her cottage. Terrific—Jonah would notice every single leak in the barn roof. And the place always looked less appealing in wet weather, because the stone walls darkened with moisture. He'd be seeing her stable at its worst.

Instead of doing housework during her extra hour of being awake, Ruth Ann decided to start early on her chores at the barn. Between five and six, she mucked out all the stalls, swept the aisles, cleaned horse hair out of the drain in the wash stall and made sure the lounge and tack room were clean and tidy.

By seven, she was exhausted.

Then the real chores started. She made up all the feed mixtures and distributed each meal to the correct horse, walked the grays out to the pasture in the rain, and brought the dark horses in for their breakfasts. The water buckets had to be emptied, washed and filled again.

Ruth Ann looked at the clock. Ten, and Jonah hadn't shown up. Damn him

She made herself a cup of coffee and sat down at the table in the lounge, but then didn't feel interested enough to take a sip. Crossing her arms in front of her, she rested her chin on her wrist…and then her cheek, as her scratchy eyes sought relief behind lowered lids. She'd only rest for a minute….

DARCY usually went straight to class from breakfast. Today, though, she'd left the literature book she would need for first period on the floor by her bed. So instead of a plate of nice hot pancakes and sausage, she settled for a jelly doughnut swallowed in gulps as she trudged up the dormitory stairs to her room.

The door was open when she got there, which ticked her off. Eve was always doing that, going off and leaving the room unlocked, like it didn't matter if someone came in and went through their stuff. She didn't seem to care if anybody knew what a mess she made, either—clothes on the floor, bed wrecked, books and papers everywhere. Eve brought food back from the dining hall, too, so there were crumbs and drips on top of everything else. Darcy wanted to scream at her for being such a slob. Did her mother let her get away with this stuff at home?

Pushing past the door, Darcy went to pick up the book, lying just where she'd left it. Then she decided she'd better go to the bathroom, so she dropped her book bag on the bed and headed for the common washroom down the hall. The dorm was quiet, for a change, with everybody heading to class.

As soon as she entered the bathroom she heard the unmistakable sound of someone throwing up. "Hey," she called. "Are you okay?" One stall door was closed. The vomiting came from there.

The retching continued, with no answer to her question. Darcy peed, then washed her hands, and the other girl still hadn't come out. "Listen, do you want me to get the nurse? Really—say something or I'm going for help."

"Just shut up, why don't you?" Eve asked, stepping out of the stall. She pulled a paper towel off the dispenser and wiped her mouth. "I'm fine."

She didn't look fine. Her eyes were red, swollen, her face white and thin. Her hair fell in strings around her face and some of them looked damp.

Darcy knew the signs. "You do this a lot, don't you?"

Eve was washing her hands. "What?"

"Throw up your food, duh. You know it's not good for you, right?"

"I know you can never be too thin." Eve looked her over, and her mouth twisted in disgust. "You should try it sometime."

Darcy's insides shriveled. "You'll make yourself sick. Really sick."

"Yeah, yeah." Tossing the paper towel into the trash, Eve headed for the exit. "Look at the bright side. I get to eat whatever I want…and wear a size zero. What's wrong with this picture? Not a damn thing."

Left alone, Darcy stared at herself in the mirror. She thought she'd probably gained a couple of pounds just since school started. The food was good, and nobody cared how much you ate. The therapist had asked her about her food choices and suggested exercise. Yeah, right. Like she'd ever put on shorts and a T-shirt and go out running with Eve—Eve, in her jogging bra and tiny shorts, with her long, thin arms and legs, her bouncy blond ponytail.

Not like me. Rolls of fat. That's what she saw when she looked in the mirror. Rolls under her chin and on her back, above the waist of her uniform skirt and below. Dough Girl, they'd called her at her last school. Somebody here would think of that, soon.

Through the mirror, she eyed the toilet stalls. That doughnut for breakfast had tasted so good. But she didn't need it now. She could survive on her own fat for months. Years, probably.

Maybe…just maybe Eve was right.

JONAH'S first appointment of the day was with his real estate agent at 8:00 a.m. He'd expected to see two or three houses and was surprised, not to mention dismayed, when the agent suggested visiting seven properties. Since he hadn't specified an exact time with Ruth Ann, Jonah went along with the agent's agenda, but as noon approached, he began to regret his decision.

"None of these houses is what I'm looking for," he said, finally. "I don't want to spend time on major renovations. I won't live in a builder's spec house, with prefabricated moldings and all the excitement of flat soda. Are there no houses with character that don't need a year's worth of work to be habitable?"

Shuffling papers, the agent looked flustered. "With the square footage you require…" He shook his head. "I've got one place left, a little ways out of town. I'll drive you over and you can see what you think."

After fifteen minutes on yet another winding road, the agent turned onto a gravel lane between broken brick pillars.

"Not a good sign," Jonah growled.

The agent sighed. On either side, scrawny pines and thin hardwood trees had taken over cleared land, with brambles and scrub underneath.

"You might as well turn—" Jonah started. And then stopped.

The house was a Victorian gem, complete with ginger-bread trim on the eaves, diamond panes in some of the windows, stained glass in others and a giant mahogany front door with its beveled-glass design intact.

"What's the history?" Jonah walked around the outside, inspecting the wood siding, the brick foundation, seeking flaws and finding very few.

"One family owned the house and passed it from generation to generation until about ten years ago, when the last survivor sold it off. It's been sold three times since—"

"Why?"

The agent shrugged as they mounted the front steps. "Seven bedrooms is too big for most folks, even families. Costs a fortune to heat, with a coal-burning furnace. No air conditioning, old-fashioned bathrooms and kitchen." He unlocked the door. "The interior is in great shape. It's just antiquated."

Home, was the word Jonah chose as he stepped inside. Polished floors in remarkably good shape stretched for what seemed like acres in every direction. Each of the four parlors on the main floor boasted a fireplace, as did the bedrooms upstairs, all in different colors of marble. Huge windows graced every wall, the crown moldings were hand-carved, the baseboards a foot deep.

Yes, the kitchen lacked a single appliance manufactured after 1970. And yes, the closest thing to a shower was a hand-held rubber hose. The coal-burning monster in the basement would have done justice to a Stephen King novel.

"I'll take it," Jonah said, climbing the steps back to the kitchen. "How soon can I take possession?"

"Uh…any time." The agent swallowed hard. "I can help you get a great interest rate on your mortgage—"

"I'll pay cash, for ten grand under the asking price."

"Well, then. Just let me call the seller."

While the agent made his call from the front porch, Jonah walked through the rooms again. As an architect, the authenticity of the house appealed to him. Very few changes had been made to the original structure and ornamentation. The setting, on a slight rise, with mountains, fields and ponds on all sides, was priceless.

But he'd based his decision to buy on a single vision that had flashed through his mind at his first glimpse of the place. He'd seen himself in an upper window—his studio, he knew, with a drawing table and bookshelves and a big leather couch—watching as children played on the lawn below. Darcy had been among them, a young woman taking care of brothers and sisters. Somewhere in the house, or out back, perhaps, was the woman who'd shared with him in creating those precious lives.

Jonah wanted to make the vision real. His parents were good people and they'd given him an adventurous, educational childhood. But despite all the traveling they'd done with him, despite his years in the best private schools and colleges in the country, despite even his marriage to Brittany and the time he'd spent in Manhattan, he had never found a place to settle and raise a family of his own. Until now.

"The sellers are delighted, of course," the agent said as he came back inside. "I'll get a contract written up and we'll go from there."

"Make the sale contingent on a home inspection," Jonah told him. He might be making an emotional purchase, but he wasn't a fool.

"Of course, of course."

By the time the formalities had been covered and Jonah could leave for Hawkridge, noon had come and gone. Today, he kept to the speed limit as he made mental notes on what he wanted done to the house before he moved in. Sitting in the parking area of Ruth Ann's stable—in reality, just a clear space under some pine trees—he entered the list into his handheld computer. Then he left the car and walked around to the front of the barn.

The dark-green double doors were closed against the weather, but the chill followed him as he stepped inside—a combination of dampness and shadows, intensified by the building's stone foundation. The main hallway, where he stood, formed the bottom of a U, with ten stalls on each arm opening into the center courtyard.

To his immediate right, the door labeled Tack was closed. On his left, the lounge door stood open slightly. Following his instincts, Jonah walked through that door into a room filled with beige. Beige walls, beige couch and chairs—not matching, simply variations on the theme—were paired with equally mismatched coffee table, side tables and lamps. The table and chairs near the beige counter had been constructed from a wood as lifeless as the rest of the room.

Ruth Ann sat at the table sound asleep, her head pillowed on her folded arms. She looked like a child, with her lashes fanned out on her pink cheeks, her shiny hair tousled, her lips soft and full. Jonah couldn't help a soft chuckle.

At the noise, she startled and sat upright with a gasp. "What—?" Then she recognized him and slapped her palms on the table top. "You scared me!"

"Sorry." Now he laughed outright, seeing the side of her face red and creased, her sleepy-eyed glare. "I didn't know this was nap time."

"It's not." She knuckled her eyes. "I was waiting for you and—and just dozed off for a minute." Swiveling on the chair, she checked the wall clock behind her. "More or less." She faced him and the glare returned. "Why are you so late? I thought you wanted to see how I worked. Half the day is over at this point."

Jonah made a small bow. "I do apologize. A business appointment in town took longer than I'd planned. But I'm here now." He gestured into the barn. "Why don't you show me around?"

Ruth Ann blinked at him, still not sure whether this was part of the dream she'd been having or not. In her dream, though, Jonah had wakened her by touching her hair, stroking her cheek. And when she'd turned to look at him, he'd bent close for a kiss….

Which meant this would definitely be reality. "Sure," she said, scraping her chair back from the table. "This is… uh…the lounge."

He nodded. "That's what the sign says." Glancing over the room, he lifted an eyebrow. "When did you last update the furniture—1960?"

"Probably. What's wrong with it?" She looked around at surroundings as familiar as her own skin. "It's been like this since my dad's day."

"I can tell. All the beige makes me feel like I'm sitting inside a mushroom. You could use a little color to liven up the place. Make the girls more comfortable."

She immediately thought of Eve, and bristled. "The girls are not here to sit in the lounge. This is a stable, Jonah. Horses are the main attraction." Walking past him, she was careful to keep her distance. "And the horses are this way."

She didn't think he would be interested in them as individuals and hadn't planned to share details with him. But he surprised her by asking questions, the answers to which seemed to involve telling him about the horses' histories, their idiosyncrasies, their talents and troubles. She showed him the work areas—wash stalls, where the horses were bathed, groomed, and saddled, then the tack room, with its rows of hangers for horses' bridles and riders' helmets, and wall racks for saddles.

Jonah examined a saddle rack. "This looks hand-tooled."

Ruth Ann stroked the smooth wood of the one closest to her. "My grandfather made them. He was quite a carpenter, as well as a horseman."

The architect's long fingers traced the base of the rack, a thick piece of oak shaped like a shield with beveled edges and the initials H and M carved into the surface, surrounded by oak leaves and acorns.

"Amazing," Jonah murmured. "So many hours of work." Fixed to the paneled wall behind it, the base supported a thick round dowel extended like an outstretched arm to hold the saddle. "Decorative and functional." He grinned at Ruth Ann. "An architect's favorite words."

"Um…" His friendliness swept her into a state of mindless panic. "The feed room's this way." Small, basic but efficient, this was the horses' "kitchen."

"Every animal has a different recipe? And they eat twice a day?" Jonah stared at the charts on her bulletin board, which listed each animal's diet. "That's a hell of a lot of detail to keep straight."

Ruth Ann shrugged. "I've been doing it my whole life, so it doesn't seem that hard. Now, ask me to design a building or decorate a room, and I'd be lost."

He grinned at her. "I noticed."

She rolled her eyes. "I like the furniture for the same reasons my dad chose it—comfort. You can sleep on that couch and never miss your bed. You can sleep in the chairs, for that matter. The table holds up your plate and glass. What else do you want?"

"Was your home the same way? Comfortable if, uh, plain?"

"No. Not really. We lived in my grandmother's house in town. Her furniture was all dark Victorian wood and velvet upholstery, with lace doilies everywhere."

"And that was okay with your dad, Mr. Beige?"

Without thinking, she elbowed Jonah in the side. "Would you stop?" But the joke only lasted a few seconds. "He stayed out here a lot of nights. He liked being able to keep an eye on the horses. I guess…" She cleared her throat. "I guess you can figure that my folks didn't have the greatest marriage. At least, not as long as I knew them." Her parents' marriage had turned bitter long before Ruth Ann had been old enough to understand what their cold silences meant.

"But they stayed together?"

"Divorce wasn't an option in their church. They remained married and tried to stay on speaking terms."

"That's hard for a kid to live with."

Ruth Ann gave a wry chuckle. "I carried messages—'Tell your father…' 'Tell your mother…'" Then she sighed. "I tried to please both of them, but it wasn't always possible."

"Did your mother ride?"

Ruth Ann shook her head. "She taught school. I don't know why she ever married Dad to begin with, since he grew up at Hawkridge, with his dad being Ridgely's stable manager. But he was a handsome devil. And she was beautiful. I guess they wanted each other too much to consider the consequences."

"That happens, unfortunately. And the kids are the ones who pay the price."

"Oh, no—I didn't mean they took it out on me. I got the best of both worlds. School with my mom and horses with my dad."

"How did you get out here? Hawkridge is a long way from town."

"Dad would pick me up and bring me out for the afternoon or weekend, then take me home again."

"So you rode with the students?"

She couldn't restrain her bark of laughter as she backed out of the feed room. "Are you kidding? I was the one saddling the horses for the students, unsaddling, brushing, washing, feeding, watering…I was the help behind the scenes while he taught the lessons."

Jonah's considering gaze rested on her face. "My mistake."

Having shown him the hay stored in two empty stalls, Ruth Ann brought him back to the front of the barn. "So there it is—my stable, and some information about how I use it. Now do you see why I think your plan won't work? You've got long distances between the tack room and the grooming areas, and a fancy lounge nobody needs. The feed room is a big waste of space and the same goes for the bathroom. We don't need the Taj Mahal. We need an efficient work area."

He nodded. "I see your points. But here's the difference between my perspective and yours. I can always redraw my plans. They're ink on paper, and that's it. Tear it up, start over."

Walking around behind her, he put his hands on her shoulders, refusing to loosen his grip when she tried to shrug free. "Now, let me show you what I see when I look at this barn of yours." He propelled her toward the north aisle of stalls. "I see three buckets down there designed to catch water from the leaky roof during this morning's rain. There are two more buckets on the other stall aisle, two in the tack room and three in the wash-stall area."

"I do need a new roof, but—"

Next, he took her to a corner of the same aisle and urged her to bend down. ' See the sawdust? Termites. You've got them all over the place, including around some supporting timbers."

She tried to shrug out from under his hands, without success. "I didn't say it was perfect."

Jonah walked her out to the yard between the stall aisles. "I can't believe crumbling brick and mortar is the safest, most beneficial surface for horses to be walking on."

"No…"

Back inside, he pointed to a tangle of extension cords going to one of the few electrical outlets. "Do I have to explain the problem here?"

She shook her head.

"Those are just the most obvious issues." They went into the lounge, where he spun her around to face him. "We won't even talk about aesthetics, although there's valid research to support the idea that a more carefully designed environment would benefit the girls' emotional states. And yours."

Ruth Ann jerked back, relieved when his hands released her. "There's nothing wrong with my emotional state. And these are all problems that could be addressed with renovations. There's nothing you've mentioned that says we need a new barn."

"You'd be putting thousands—tens of thousands, probably—of dollars into a hundred-year-old building."

"People do that all the time, for historic buildings they want to preserve."

"It's a barn, Ruth Ann, with dirt floors in the stalls and plumbing a century out of date. Primitive electrical wiring. Ceiling beams that have been leaked on for decades, no doubt. Your dad probably put the same buckets under the same bloody leaks."

She didn't—couldn't—answer him.

"So do you think those beams are still structurally sound? And do you think the leaks you see are the only ones that exist? My guess is there's rot in the walls, including the supporting timbers. Who knows when a piece of the roof will come down on you or a horse…or a kid?"

He shoved his hands into the pockets of his slacks. "I appreciate your history with this place. But the girls deserve more—and that's my job. My professional and personal opinion is that we need to design a new stable for The Hawkridge School. Not the plan I drew, maybe, but that's a start. We need to build a new barn…

"…and tear this one down to the ground."

Chapter Six

Ruth Ann looked as if she'd been socked in the gut—or kicked by a horse. Her face went white, her lips parted and her jaw hung loose.

She stood motionless so long, Jonah began to worry. He put out a hand, touched her arm. "Ruth Ann—"

"Get out." She squared her shoulders and straightened her spine. Her chin came up. "Get out," she said again, her voice loud and harsh. "I don't want you in my barn. I don't want you near my horses."

She shoved at his shoulder with the heel of her hand. Then she marched past him and threw the door open, waiting with obvious impatience for him to leave. As Jonah crossed the threshold, she surprised him with a final push that sent him stumbling forward. Catching his balance on a nearby pine tree, he heard a slam which sent a message all its own.

Back in the Porsche, he headed for the Manor. He would have to tell Jayne Thomas what he'd decided, what he'd "accomplished" today—the complete alienation of Ruth Ann Blakely. If Miriam and her board of directors wanted a new barn, he had a feeling they'd have to build it in the face of the equestrian trainer's opposition. From what he knew of Ruth Ann, he didn't expect her to back down.

But neither would he. "The place is marginally safe," he told the headmistress a few minutes later. "I'm sure Ruth Ann is careful with the girls and the horses, vigilant about lights and electricity. But it's an old stable. Renovation, in this case, would be essentially the same as building new, in terms of cost and time invested."

Jayne clasped her hands on her desk. "Did you say this to Ruth Ann?"

"I was quite blunt." He felt increasingly guilty about just how blunt he'd been. "I thought I could shock her into a recognition of how truly hopeless the place is."

"That sounds…risky."

He nodded. "She threw me out. Bodily."

"Oh."

"Right. She's mad as hell." As Jayne sighed, he said, "She did show me around the place first, though, and pointed out some errors in my plan. I can rework the design, incorporating what I've learned from Ruth Ann. Maybe she'll recognize the effort, and come around."

"I doubt it. Her childhood is there. She idolized her father, and that's where she spent time with him. We're not going to change any of that. But you've only confirmed my own opinion—Hawkridge needs a newer, safer stable."

Jayne got to her feet. "So why don't you do some revising on your plans, and we'll schedule another meeting when you've got something to show? I'll work on softening up Ruth Ann. Surely she can be brought to see good sense."

"I hope so." As he left the administrative offices, Jonah glanced across the black and white marble-floored entry hall and found Darcy sitting halfway up the circular staircase, alone, with a book open in her lap. Instead of reading or working, though, her chin rested in her hands, and she was staring off into space.

Jonah hesitated, then thought, *To hell with the rules.*

"Hi, Darcy." He climbed toward her, weaving a path through the girls occupying space on the steps as Darcy was. "Shouldn't you be in class?"

"I have a free period."

She looked around with a worried expression, as if they might be caught doing something illegal. "What are you doing here?"

"I came by to talk to Ms. Thomas, and then I saw you up here and thought I'd say hello. Can you walk me out to the car?"

After casing the joint again, she nodded. Outside, Jonah saw her shoulders relax and her head come up. But he waited until they'd reached the Porsche before saying anything.

"How's it going? Do you like your classes?"

One shoulder lifted in a shrug. "Pretty much. English Lit is really good. Algebra, not so much."

"Are you getting to know some of the girls?"

"A little."

"Is Eve as big a pain as I thought she would be?"

Darcy laughed. "More. She's a slob and a snob."

"Unbearable?"

The laugh died away. "Not really. She's not in the room much. She spends a lot of time at the gym."

He wanted to ask if she could be happy at Hawkridge, if she wanted to leave, if this was the right decision. But how could Darcy answer those questions?

So he kept things simple. "Well, I just wanted to say hi. You'd better get back, get your homework done before dinner. Is the food good?"

"Really good." It was the first enthusiasm she'd shown over anything. "They have fantastic desserts."

"Well, then, enjoy." He knew Brittany would have said exactly the opposite. But he thought Darcy just needed some kind of fun exercise to use up the calories, rather than simply limiting them. She was a kid. Kids shouldn't have to diet.

His own stomach rumbled with hunger. Breakfast was only a distant memory. Driving out to Hawkridge, he'd thought he might talk Ruth Ann into having dinner with him in town somewhere.

"You blew that one," he told himself, putting the car into gear. "After this morning, you'll be lucky if the woman doesn't clean her stalls and then empty her wheelbarrow into the trunk of your car!"

But Jonah didn't intend to give up. He would have a drawing table installed in his new house within a matter of days. Then he'd begin reworking the barn project.

Ruth Ann might be stubborn, but she wasn't stupid. He'd shocked her this morning, but now she could begin to realize she did need a better facility. When she admitted that fact, he'd be ready with a plan which took her working style and requirements into account. She wouldn't quit her job, because she'd be so in love with his design she couldn't bear to leave it.

And he would secure the contract that allowed him to resign from the firm in New York and set up his own business right here in Ridgeville.

All he had to do was play smart, and both of them would get exactly what they wanted.

BY THE TIME her lesson kids started showing up that afternoon, Ruth Ann had worked off her temper. At least enough to act normally with the girls, she hoped.

Then Ingrid came into the lounge and looked around. "Wow—what happened in here?"

"I just cleaned up a little, that's all." To be accurate, she'd scrubbed every surface in the room, except for the ceiling.

"You can see the faces in the pictures now," Ingrid said, gazing at framed photographs hanging on the wall. "You look like your dad, don't you?"

"Unfortunately." Ruth Ann pulled the last out-of-date yogurt carton from the refrigerator and threw it in the trash can. "He was handsome, but a little short for a guy. I'm the same height and tall for a woman. Go figure."

Two more students came in and exclaimed over the cleanliness of the room. Then one of them bounced down onto the sofa. "The couch still stinks, anyway," she said. The three girls laughed.

"Okay, get tacked up," Ruth Ann told them. "Your rides are on the bulletin board. If you're not in the saddle at four o'clock, I have some stalls you can clean."

When the girls were gone, Ruth Ann sat on the sofa, and then lay down with her face in the cushions. Yes, she supposed the couch did smell old, a little musty, a little like horses and dirt, though she'd never noticed it before. Of course, on the unusual occasions when she slept here—sick or injured horses, bad storms, loss of electric service—she was so exhausted she wouldn't be aware if the couch collapsed underneath her.

So maybe her dad's furniture ought to be replaced. Did she have the cash to throw away on new chairs? Not hardly. And, anyway, dark beige was a nice, neutral color. Went with everything. Didn't show dirt.

Just smelled like it.

Half an hour later, Ruth Ann was standing in the arena, watching Ingrid and the other girls practice a sitting trot, when Darcy appeared at the back door of the barn. As the lesson progressed, Darcy worked her way toward the ring until she was sitting on one of the spectators' benches.

Seeing her reminded Ruth Ann of the Architect from Hell, as she'd decided to call him, according to whose "professional and personal opinion," she should destroy the Hawkridge stable.

This building had been the center of her dad's life—not the house in Ridgeville where they'd slept, eaten breakfast and dinner, gotten baths and clean clothes. Here he'd been able to share himself with her. Leaving this barn would mean losing her dad all over again.

"Ooooowwww! Ms. Blakely! Please, can we stop?"

She came out of her thoughts to find all three of her students wilting over their horses' necks. She'd left them trotting without stirrups for quite a long time.

And they'd be all the stronger for the pain. "Sure," she called. "Now that you're warmed up, let me see some canter circles, still without stirrups. Be sure to keep the horse nicely bent, on the bridle, and sit deep in the saddle."

More groans greeted her direction as she left the dressage arena and walked toward Darcy. "How are you this afternoon?"

As usual, Darcy shrugged. "Okay." Her gaze never left the horses. "Riding without stirrups is hard."

Ruth Ann sat down beside her. "Some people learn to ride without ever using stirrups at all. Then it seems easy. It's all a matter of balance and strength."

"I always get wobbly."

"You need more practice." As the sun came out from behind a cloud, she noticed that Darcy's face looked pinched and pale in the afternoon light. "Are you feeling okay?"

"Sure."

She stifled the urge to touch the girl's forehead to see if she might have a fever. "Have you been eating pretty well?"

"I love the food." Darcy crossed her arms over her waist and hugged tight. After a long pause, she said, "What do you think of...throwing up?"

"I hate it," Ruth Ann said. "Means I'm sick and my stomach hurts and it's really gross." She understood what Darcy really wanted to know, but if she wanted an answer, then she would have to be frank about the question.

After another long pause, Darcy said, "I mean, on purpose."

"Ah." Ruth Ann faced the arena. "I *know* it's a bad idea. Your body doesn't function well when you abuse it like that."

"But you get to eat whatever you want to. And still be thin."

"Until you do so much damage that you can't eat even if you want to, and then you get really sick."

"I can't stand eating just salad all the time. I don't like lettuce."

"Me, neither. It doesn't have much taste."

"And it's cold. Most of the skinny foods are cold. Sometimes, you need something warm to—to make you feel better, you know?"

"I do know." Ruth Ann blinked back tears. "I like macaroni and cheese casserole. And buttered toast."

"I like baked potatoes with butter and sour cream and cheese." Darcy's arms loosened a little from around her waist.

"Yeah." Ruth Ann turned slightly to brace her elbow on the back of the bench and rest her head in her hand. "One answer is to eat food that's good for you. Not just salad, but lots of veggies, lean meats, whole grain bread, not so many sweets. Another option, for people who really like to eat, is exercise. Use up the calories."

"I hate exercise. Running, sit-ups, jumping jacks, stair-climbing—yuck. I just feel worse, and then I go eat more."

"From what I've seen, I think there is one exercise you enjoy."

"Walking? No, I hate that, too. I only walked here because that's the way to see the horses."

"Exactly."

The girl thought about it for a minute. "You mean riding could be my exercise?"

"Why not?"

"It doesn't feel like hard work."

"For people who enjoy it—which does not include me, by the way—running isn't hard work. The secret is to find something you like to do that will make you stronger, use your muscles and your lungs and your heart."

"But how does riding do that?"

She stood up. "Come with me." To the girls in the arena, she called, "Ingrid, Karen, Marne, that's good. Start cooling down."

Standing with Darcy just outside the rail, Ruth Ann said, "Okay, the horses have been cantering around. They're breathing fast, because they've been working. What do you notice about the riders?"

Eyes narrowed, Darcy stared. "They're sweaty. Breathing hard."

"Because cantering without stirrups is hard work. They've used thigh muscles and butt muscles and stomach muscles to stay on. They had to move with the horse, so their heart and lungs got a workout, too."

Darcy turned with her to walk back to the barn. Ruth Ann went on. "Before they got on the horse, the girls had to groom the animal and tack up—that's bending and stretching. Karen had to retrieve Sheba from the pasture—she used calories walking out there and back. Now they'll untack, brush the horses and put away their gear. Ingrid will help me for the next couple of hours by cleaning stalls—great for your arm and back muscles, plus it uses more calories. Do you see? If being around horses is something you love, then you can exercise and not even care about how hard it is. I call it the Manure Diet."

"The Manure Diet?" To Ruth Ann's surprise, Darcy giggled. "That's gross."

"Not as gross as throwing up after every meal. Plus, you get stronger, and you ride better."

"Could I really do that? I mean, I fall off so much."

Ruth Ann forgot to be cautious about touching. She put her hands on the girl's shoulders and looked directly into her face. "I'm not going to lie to you. Everybody falls off a horse if they ride long enough. It's a fact of nature that even the very best riders can't avoid.

"But it's not because they're clumsy. There might be good reasons why you fell off and broke your arm. Maybe you didn't have enough experience for the horse you were riding. Maybe he was in a bad mood that day. Or he got scared, and you didn't think fast enough about what he would do next."

"I couldn't think, period. All I could do was try to hold onto the reins. And even that didn't work."

Ruth Ann nodded. "Been there, done that. But the one thing that can keep you safer on the horse—any horse—is learning how to ride. Practice so often that your body reacts before you have to think about it, and that way you fall off a lot less often. You need experience, Darcy. Experience, and some belief in yourself."

For a long moment, Darcy stood absolutely still, staring inward. The three older girls walked by, leading their horses to the barn to be unsaddled.

Finally, her gaze connected with Ruth Ann's. "Can I start today? Can you show me how?"

INGRID and Darcy left at 6:00 p.m. Darcy had cleaned two stalls by herself, working around Ruth Ann's gentlest and most tolerant horses, Dusty and George. Then Darcy had walked the two geldings out to the field by herself, a big accomplishment for one day. After so much exercise, Ruth Ann felt confident the girl would not purge after dinner tonight.

With the barn to herself again, Ruth Ann walked the aisles, checking the door locks and water buckets, making sure all the horses had enough hay before she left for supper. Her father had followed the same routine, and his father before him.

The smell and the feel of this barn, the sound of her footsteps on the stone floor, her intimate knowledge of every idiosyncratic lock and hinge and, yes, leak…how could she give those up? Why would anyone expect her to, even the AFH?

After visiting all the horses, she walked back to the lounge. The unexpected sight of someone waiting for her at the table made her jump.

"Jayne! Damn, you scared me. Why didn't you let me know you were here?" In the first instant, she'd thought Jonah had returned. Awareness of her disappointment made her angry with herself…and him, all over again.

"I just sat down," Jayne said, "after making us some tea. Join me."

Ruth Ann complied, but gave her friend a questioning look. "I need a cup of tea to hear what you're going to say?"

"Maybe." The headmistress took a sip from her own mug. "Jonah stopped by to talk to me after he saw you today. It sounds like he was pretty hard on you."

"Did he say that?"

"More or less. But he holds by his opinion—he believes Hawkridge needs a new facility in order to continue offering equestrian skills as part of our curriculum."

The formal language seemed to put the conversation on a different level, especially when Jayne went on. "Our insurance provider and attorney would no doubt agree. Liability is an issue we can't afford to ignore, Ruth Ann."

"No one has ever been injured in my barn or by my barn. Or my horses. The falls we have are minor, because I'm careful to match the horses to the girls' skill levels. I supervise constantly. I—"

"I know, I know," Jayne said in a soothing voice. "But suppose you aren't here?"

"Why wouldn't I be?" Though she'd threatened to get a different job, she really couldn't visualize her life anywhere besides Hawkridge.

"You could decide to change careers, or get married and move away."

Ruth Ann snorted a laugh. "Not likely."

"Anything's possible. And maybe we get an instructor who isn't as careful, as wise as you."

"If you hire someone who doesn't look out for the girls, no beautiful new barn is going to prevent accidents."

"Of course not." Jayne closed her eyes for a second. "Look, I'm sure you've got a counter for every reason I offer. I'm not saying you don't have valid arguments on your side."

Ruth Ann nodded at the newly cleaned pictures on the wall beside her. "Are we just going to throw away the history this barn has seen? Presidents, senators and tycoons toured the Hawkridge estate on horseback with Howard and Agatha Ridgely. They all used this barn. The Queen of England visited to inspect a pair of carriage horses she wanted to buy, horses bred and trained right here by my granddad."

"I know."

"So, why can't Jonah Granger design something else for the school and leave me and my horses alone?"

"Because the Board of Directors is convinced we need this new stable—"

"Because Miriam brainwashed them."

Jayne's wince conceded the point. "I'm really worried that a showdown between you and Miriam will end badly for you...and for me. I don't want to get another trainer and instructor. I'd love for us both to be teaching at Hawkridge twenty years from now. But the balance of power is not in your favor, Ruth Ann."

Looking at her friend, Ruth Ann suddenly saw the whole truth. "If you came out on my side, defied Miriam and the board, they might very well fire you, too."

Jayne shrugged. "I think the possibility exists. The problem is, I don't think I can come down solidly on your side, with regard to the barn. It's a nice old building, but..." She smiled apologetically. "I think we need a new stable, too."

"So why are you here?"

"To ask you to cooperate." Reaching across the table, she put her hand over Ruth Ann's fist. "I'd really appreciate it if you'd work with Jonah Granger, not against him. He's committed to drawing up new plans, based on what he saw with you today."

"Terrific."

"I'd like you to have an open mind about what he brings to the table, to share what you think would improve the project. We're not asking you to agree blindly. We want your experienced perspective on the project."

"And to ignore the fact that you're ripping my heart out?"

"Oh, Ruth Ann." Now both of Jayne's hands covered hers. "I'm sorry you feel that way. But change is a part of life, sweetie. You'd have more than a year before the new construction would be ready. I believe you can accustom yourself in that time and begin looking forward to a new place to work."

She got to her feet. "Think how much easier your job will be when the roof doesn't leak. When the floors are level and smooth, the stall latches don't have to be jiggled exactly the right way to function and the doors shut tight no matter what the weather." Walking toward the door, she put a hand on Ruth Ann's shoulder for a moment. "And maybe, just maybe, we can find the salary for at least one extra worker for the stable in Miriam's donation. How's that for incentive?"

Jayne didn't wait for the answer, but let herself out while Ruth Ann was still thinking…and Ruth Ann sat thinking as the sun set and the lounge got dark. Her head could see Jayne's point. Her heart just cried. She didn't know which would get its way.

Chapter Seven

Jonah scheduled a meeting with the Hawkridge Board of Directors for the middle of October. Jayne Thomas assured him Ruth Ann would attend, as well. That gave him five weeks to revise his barn plan while supervising his two other projects and getting the new house organized.

He soon realized a full night's sleep would not be part of his agenda. Singlehandedly managing three very different design operations required an efficiency he had always produced without effort. These days, though, unless he was working on the Hawkridge stable, he had to force himself to concentrate. Atlanta and Charlotte didn't seem nearly as important in the scheme of things as this small private school in western North Carolina.

Because of Darcy, maybe. Even when he did lie down on the couch at three or four in the morning—his bed was on back order at the factory—he didn't sleep soundly. He spent a lot of time remembering the look of betrayal in Ruth Ann's golden eyes when he'd recommended tearing down her barn. He hadn't simply attacked a building, he'd realized since. He had committed a personal assault, one she did not deserve.

So, on the last Sunday in September, when he was certain

there would be no furniture deliveries and no construction emergencies, he got into his truck and headed out to Hawkridge. Maybe if he apologized, he could get Ruth Ann off his mind.

He drove with the windows down, letting the crisp, cool air blow through his hair and, he hoped, his brain. The weather had been dry and the trees were starting to take on their fall colors—the dark, green-blue slopes of summer had given way to greenish-gold and orange, with occasional splashes of red and yellow. Bright sun and a brilliant blue sky had replaced the usual smoky mist. Though New Englanders bragged about their autumns, Jonah was beginning to think he preferred the Smokies.

The Hawkridge barn seemed very quiet when he arrived. On such a beautiful afternoon, he would have expected every horse-crazy student to have come out for a ride. He couldn't see any sign of equestrian activity. Maybe Ruth Ann took Sundays off?

With disappointment lurking at the back of his mind, Jonah left the truck and walked around to the front of the stable. The big green doors stood open—a good sign.

He stepped inside. "Ruth Ann? Anybody here?"

"Stall fourteen," she called. "In the back." A sound he hadn't registered until that moment started up again—the slide of a shovel blade against earth.

Horses poked their heads out of the stalls as he passed, and Jonah petted each one as he made his way to the end of the aisle where an open door revealed Ruth Ann standing with a shovel in hand and half the floor of the stall missing.

"What's wrong?" Jonah asked.

"What are you doing here?" she demanded at the same time.

They glared at each other for a moment, until he remembered why he'd come. "I came to apologize," Jonah said, deliberately dowsing the flare of his temper. "What are you doing?"

"What does it look like? I'm taking out the floor."

"Why?"

She took a deep breath and blew it out again. "Because a horse has been peeing and pooping on it." She spoke slowly, as if to a child who wasn't too bright. "Horse pee smells bad and grows bacteria. I dig out the clay floor, replace it with fresh so the stall is clean and the horses stay healthy." Aiming her shovel, she prepared to dig again. "Now, if that's all…"

"No, it's not." Jonah leaned a shoulder against the door frame. "Do you dig out twenty stalls by yourself?"

"No. I usually borrow a couple of guys from maintenance at the school to help me. But they don't work on Sunday and I want to get this finished." She put her foot on the shoulder of the shovel.

"No girls around to help today?"

"It's, um, my day off."

"Looks like it." He chuckled. "Wouldn't this be a hell of lot easier with a backhoe or a tractor?"

Ruth Ann rolled her eyes. "The short answer is yes."

"The long answer is…?"

She flashed him an angry glance. "The doors were built before machines like that were available. They're too narrow."

"Ah." He swallowed his smile.

This time she didn't try to resume digging. "Any other questions?"

"Got another shovel?"

Her jaw dropped. "You are not coming in here to dig."

"Why not?"

"Because—" She shook her head. "Because I don't want you to."

Jonah walked to the stall's exterior door, where he found

two more shovels leaning against the outside wall. "You don't need help?" he asked over his shoulder.

"This is not your job."

"You don't think I can shovel well enough?"

"There's no reason for you to get filthy."

He turned and looked her straight in the eye. "You don't think I owe you some kind of reparations for what I said the last time I was here?"

Ruth Ann didn't reply.

Holding the shovel in one hand, Jonah made a halting motion with the other. "I'm not saying I was wrong, mind you. I do think you need a more efficient and functional stable. But I shouldn't have discounted the worth of this building to you personally. I'm sorry about that."

Staring at him, Ruth Ann didn't know which of her warring impulses would win. Any sane woman would want to keep this man working nearby, just for the pleasure of watching him move. Worn, well-fitting jeans showed off his strong legs. The view when he'd leaned out to get the shovel had nearly given her palpitations. Now he was rolling back the sleeves on his chambray shirt to reveal well-shaped forearms, which looked plenty capable of handling a shovelful of clay with ease.

But how could she allow her arch-enemy to help her with this job—the AFH himself stripping her stall? What had happened to her pride, her self-sufficiency?

Jonah's apology had been appropriate, and seemed sincere. He understood what this place meant to her. But he wasn't beyond using this kind of work as a weapon, trying to convince her to accept the new plan.

To give him credit, though, he hadn't just barged into the work. He was standing with his arms folded on the handle of the shovel, waiting for her decision. "Well?" he said, lifting one straight, black eyebrow.

"Oh, suit yourself," Ruth Ann told him. "It's your aching back."

They worked for a while in a silence broken by only the rasp of metal blades against dirt and the occasional grunt or curse from one of them. Ruth Ann tried not to glance at the man beside her, at the play of muscles under those jeans, the stretch of cotton cloth over his shoulders, more than once every ten—okay, five—minutes.

"It's a good thing the weather's turned cool," Jonah commented after awhile. "This would be miserable work in the summer or winter."

Panting with effort, she nodded. "And in the spring, we get rain."

"Is this the last stall or the first?"

"You don't want to know."

"I was afraid you'd say that."

They both huffed a laugh and kept working. Ruth Ann reached the end wall first, and began to dig along that edge. As she reached the outside corner, she noticed splinters of wood coming away from the wall with the clay. Gritting her teeth, she kept digging, careful not to hit the boards if she could help it.

Once she had excavated on both sides of the corner, though, the truth was hard to ignore. When she stuck the point of the shovel into the boards below ground level, they broke into soggy crumbles surrounded by piles of sawdust. She didn't have to bend close to see thousands of insects crawling over, under and through the destroyed wood.

"Jonah."

He stopped shoveling and turned to look at what she'd done. Then he clucked his tongue. "Yeah. Termites."

Ruth Ann swallowed hard. "How much damage do you suppose they've done?"

"Step back."

She didn't question the order. Coming forward with his shovel, Jonah hit the wall just as she had done, and they both watched it crumble. By the time he'd finished, a hole four by five feet had opened up at the bottom of that wall, and another one half that size on the other side of the corner.

"That corner post is a supporting structure," he said. "I don't want to disturb it because it's holding up the roof. But chances are it's rotten, too."

"Terrific." Ruth Ann threw her shovel down. "There's no sense in finishing this stall, because I can't leave a horse in here now." She pulled in a deep breath. "Thanks for your help, Jonah. I'll take it from here."

"Take it where?"

"It's a figure of speech. You're free to go. It's getting late and I have to get the horses fed, the other stalls cleaned."

"What are you going to do about these walls?"

She rubbed her forehead with the back of her hand. "I'm not sure. I guess...I guess I'll get the maintenance guys to bring in some boards, replace the ones that have disintegrated and brace the rest somehow."

"You know the whole building could have defects like this?"

"Yes, I know. But I can only handle one defect at a time."

"You should get an inspection. Would the school pay for termite treatment?"

She laughed at him. "Are you kidding? With your new stable plan hanging out there like a carrot in front of a donkey's nose, I'll probably have to cover the cost of the repairs myself. They won't want to spend money on this barn when there's a new one in the works."

"Where will the horse in this stall go?"

"I consolidated the hay stalls, so I can use one of those during the cleaning process. Of course, that will cut down on the amount of hay I can store for the winter." Suddenly, the ramifications of the problem appeared endless. "Hay gets more expensive in the winter, so my feed bills will go up just when the grass dies out and they're eating more. I'll have to justify the increase to the board, and the board will get all snotty about it." She sighed. "But I guess I can handle snotty."

"I'm sure of it." Jonah leaned his shovel against the stall wall. "If you tell me how I can help you feed the horses, you can be out of here faster."

But that was where the dam holding back Ruth Ann's temper broke. "Don't do me any favors!" she told him loudly.

He gazed at her in surprise. "What's wrong now?"

"You don't get it, do you? Nobody gets it. I don't want to be 'out of here,' faster or otherwise. I like being at the barn. I like being with the horses. God knows they're more dependable than any human being I've ever known."

"Ruth Ann—"

"I don't mind staying late, working long hours. This isn't my job—this is my *life*."

She expected him to give up at that point, to throw his hands up in surrender, stalk out to his car and drive off. Most guys she knew would. The few men she'd dated had.

Jonah just glared at her. "And you don't see a problem with that?"

"No," she threw back at him. "I don't."

"You're a healthy, attractive woman in the prime of her life and all you can think about is taking care of your horses and this crumbling old barn?" He cast an exasperated glance at the ceiling. "What about a family, Ruth Ann—a human family? Children of your own? A husband? Are you so tired at the end of a day with your horses that you don't need somebody to talk to, to listen to and share with? A warm body next to yours in bed?"

He took a step toward her. "What about sex, Ruth Ann? What about this?"

While he was still speaking, Jonah grabbed her shoulders and jerked her body close to his. Then his hands framed her face and held her still, so he could claim her mouth with his.

I'm filthy, she thought. *I had onions for lunch and didn't brush my teeth. I—*

He was delicious, with a taste like dark chocolate and mint, a hint of coffee, a drop of some fiery liqueur. Orange, maybe peach. His lips were smooth, flexible, talented. She'd never known that kisses worked this way, that there was more to the game than just skin pressing hard against skin.

And, oh, she wanted to learn the skill. Wanted to practice with him until she mastered every small detail. She demonstrated what she'd learned so far, and Jonah groaned deep in his chest. His hands dropped to her shoulders and stroked down to her elbows, then his arms came around her hard and tight. For the first time she could remember, she felt small. Feminine.

Weak. Foolish. Giving in to Jonah now would make it that much harder to hold out against him in the fight for her barn.

Ruth Ann clenched her fists against his chest, stiffened her spine and leaned back, pulling away from yet another mesmerizing kiss. Jonah's arms loosened, but instead of stopping, he took the kisses from her lips to her cheeks, her eyes and her chin, which was almost as devastating.

"It's okay," he murmured over her ear. "You're safe. I've got you."

"No." She took a deep breath. "You don't." Pushing him away, she stepped back.

Jonah stood motionless for a long time, staring at her as the haze of desire cleared from his eyes and his face hardened. At last, he took a deep breath. "You're right. The situation is complicated and what just happened didn't make anything better. My apologies, yet again." Walking past her, he stepped up onto the aisle outside the stall. "See you at the meeting in October."

A late-afternoon wind blew through the barn as he left, rattling leaves against the walls and stirring the horses from their before-dinner naps. In the distance, a truck engine started, came closer, then diminished in volume as Jonah left.

Ruth Ann climbed stiffly out of the stall and started toward the feed room, feeling older than a mere thirty-three. After singlehandedly moving two hundred bales of hay yesterday, her muscles had protested the heavy work of shoveling wet clay from the moment she'd started this morning. She had wanted the work to distract her from her thoughts, though…only to have the very subject of those thoughts show up in person and proceed to demolish all her defenses. Heaven only knew what would have happened if she hadn't balked when she did.

She simply couldn't afford to leave herself vulnerable where Jonah Granger was concerned. Where any man was concerned. Her parents had been a perfect example of the way lust could make two people miserable—wanting each other and yet unable to live together in any kind of peace. She and Jonah would be just like that—the slick New York architect and the tomboy horse trainer. They had almost nothing in common, except for an interest in Darcy's welfare. The most important things in her life were obstacles to his success, and vice versa.

So there would be no more kisses from Jonah, Ruth Ann

decided. Their encounters would be strictly business from now on. Maybe she should just give in on the barn scheme, so he'd leave her alone. Then, in a year, when they'd finished the new stable, she could take her horses and find a new home. A new job. A new life.

Going through her nightly routine, feeding and taking care of her best friends, Ruth Ann couldn't find much comfort in that vision of her future.

AFTER THE giant mistake of kissing Ruth Ann Blakely, Jonah drove furiously to his new house, then drove himself furiously for the next two weeks. Speed, work and exhaustion were the only escapes he could find from the backlash of that day.

Guilt—he had plenty. He'd goaded her into that embrace. And if she hadn't resisted, God only knew where they'd have ended up. He'd certainly had no thought of stopping…kissing Ruth Ann was the best thing that had happened to him in years. Decades, maybe. The fit of her body against his, the shape of her strong, womanly curves under his hands…

Frustration—definitely, when he reached the point in his recollections when what he wanted more than anything else was…well, more. More of her spicy, peppery, passionate taste against his mouth, on his tongue. Ruth Ann's kisses were as unpredictable, as explosive, as the woman herself. And yet he'd sensed an underlying sweetness, a vulnerability he wanted to explore, to protect. Someone had hurt her, left her uncertain underneath all that strength.

Which brought him to remorse. Big-time. Jonah didn't start what he couldn't finish. But where could he and Ruth Ann go together? Would she surrender on the issue of the barn? He seriously doubted that would be the outcome of this process, no matter how hard he worked to create a design she would approve. Nothing he could do, no stable he could draw, would be good enough, because she already had what was, in her mind, the best. He was, in essence, competing with her father. How could he win against a memory?

But while Ruth Ann wouldn't give in, Jonah fully expected the Hawkridge board to approve his plan for a new barn. On a professional level, he and Ruth Ann would remain opponents, if not outright enemies. A man had no business kissing his opponent.

No matter how much he wanted to.

DARCY had figured out that she couldn't get to the second floor by the main staircase during the mad rush to lunch. The wave of girls coming down was simply too powerful to resist. Instead, she left her first-floor literature class and headed for the small, twisting stairwell beyond the dining hall. Servants would have used this staircase in a mansion like this, staying out of their employers' way.

And that was what Darcy wanted, to stay out of everyone's way as she headed toward the infirmary. Her mission there was private. She definitely didn't want any of the other girls to suspect.

Mrs. Ryan, the big Irish nurse who ran the health clinic, ate her lunch in the teachers' lounge at eleven-thirty. According to Darcy's observations, she usually returned to her desk about twelve-fifteen. Class ended at noon, so there should be a fifteen-minute window in which Darcy could get to the infirmary and out without anyone watching. She hoped.

When she reached the hallway where she should turn, she lingered a moment. Not a girl in sight—they'd all run like lemmings over a cliff to lunch. No teachers, either. She could hear them, through the open door of the lounge behind her, talking and laughing, rustling papers.

So far, so good. Walking on her toes, Darcy moved toward the infirmary. The door was shut.

Either Mrs. Ryan was gone, or Mrs. Ryan was taking a nap. Was it locked? What if she couldn't get in?

Her hand shook as she reached for the knob, which slipped out of her sweaty fingers when she tried to turn it. Wiping her palm on her skirt, Darcy took a firm grip.

Not locked! With a quick glance to each side, she put herself on the other side of the door and closed it behind her. No one walking by would know she was here.

The object of her quest stood on the other side of the room. With a deep breath, Darcy put down her books, slipped off her sweater and shoes. Now was the point of real danger. How would she explain if Mrs. Ryan came in right now?

Holding her breath, she crossed the floor to stand in front of the scale. When she stepped onto the platform, it wiggled a little under her stockinged feet. Did air weigh a lot? Should she breathe out? Would that make a difference?

She slid the weight on the bottom bar to one hundred. Maybe someday. She'd weighed in during her first week at Hawkridge—everybody did. She knew what the scale had said then, remembered Nurse Ryan shaking her head.

"Fewer cookies, more celery would be a good thing," she'd said.

Darcy had gone back to her room in tears. Today, she pushed the weight on the upper bar over quickly, wanting to get the worst over. Forty-eight had been the top number. Added to the bottom number, it told a terrible story.

But today, things had changed. With the top weight sitting on forty-eight, the bar tipped down. Too heavy!

Darcy let out her breath. She'd lost weight!

How much?

She inched the weight down a pound, then two, and three, four, five…six. The top weight sat at forrty-two! She'd lost six pounds in a month!

Now she was crying because she was so happy. Jumping off the scale, she stepped into her shoes and picked up her books, ready to hurry down to lunch. But with the door open, she remembered—she had to reset the weights on the scale.

Just as she turned toward the door again, footsteps sounded in the hallway outside.

Then a voice. "Now, I know I left that door closed. What's going on here?" Carrying her big black purse and a folded brown paper bag, Mrs. Ryan entered the infirmary.

She stopped when she saw Darcy standing in the middle of the room. "Did you have an appointment?"

"Um…no, ma'am." Darcy couldn't get to the door because Mrs. Ryan still stood there.

"Are you aware that you aren't supposed to enter the infirmary unless I'm here?"

"N-No, ma'am. I'm new this year. I—I didn't know."

"Well, now you do." The nurse walked over to her desk, leaving the doorway open for Darcy. "What do you need?" She put down her purse and the bag, then turned and picked up Darcy's wrist to take her pulse.

"I—"

"Headache? Cramps? Do you have a fever?" She held up a finger as she stared at her watch. "Your pulse is normal." Placing a hand on Darcy's forehead, Mrs. Ryan closed her eyes for a second. "You don't feel hot. Well, what is it? Why are you here?"

Darcy focused, came up with an excuse. "Headache. I do have a headache. Could I get some pain reliever?"

"Of course, dear." Mrs. Ryan went into the next room, returning with a small paper cup containing two pills and a larger one with water. "Here we are."

"Thank you." Darcy swallowed the pills without gagging, as she usually did.

"You're welcome. If it's not better in two hours, come back to see me."

"Yes, ma'am."

And then, finally, she escaped. She danced down the hallway and ran down the big staircase, cleared of all obstruction now that lunch had started. The whole world seemed bigger, brighter, than it had just fifteen minutes ago. Six whole pounds!

She found an empty seat next to girls she didn't know and surveyed the food options. Meals were served family-style, with bowls and platters of food being passed around the table. As always, a big glass bowl of salad sat in the center. On one side, Darcy could see a basket of hoagie rolls and a platter of submarine sandwich meats—roast beef, turkey, ham, pastrami—and cheese slices. Another bowl held small bags of chips. On the other side of the salad, a giant pan that had obviously been full now held only three squares of spaghetti casserole. Beyond sat a plate of buttered garlic bread. And a plate of brownies.

Darcy nodded. The Hawkridge kitchen made excellent spaghetti.

Her right hand twitched, yearning to reach out and grab two of those spaghetti squares. And a brownie. Of course, a sub would be good, too, with piles of meat and cheese, lots of mayonnaise. Darcy loved a good sub.

"What would you like to drink?" one of the serving staff asked over her shoulder.

"Just water," Darcy said automatically. She'd been drinking

water almost exclusively since Ms. Blakely had pointed out that water had no calories and made your skin look better.

She surveyed the lunch options again, and nudged the girl on her right with her elbow. "Pass the casserole, please."

Without pausing in the conversation she was having with the girl on her other side, Darcy's neighbor handed over the pan. Darcy took one square of casserole, and stood up to put the pan back in place. Then she spooned up enough of the salad to cover the rest of her plate, dousing it with vinegar and a small shake of olive oil.

The spaghetti was every bit as good as usual, and the salad had a nice crunch. Even if she hadn't been going to work at the barn this afternoon, Darcy felt she'd made a good choice. She couldn't eat just salad, or else she'd end up pigging out on brownies because she felt deprived. This way, she wouldn't be hungry until dinner.

Six pounds, she crowed to herself. *I'm six pounds lighter!*

She deserved a reward. That's what the weight-loss Web sites she'd been visiting would say. Something important, something to make herself feel wonderful for her accomplishment, something that would motivate her to keep going. What should she choose?

The vision that came into her head made Darcy gasp. Could she? Was it too soon? Was six pounds enough, or should she wait until ten? Twenty?

Ms. Blakely would give her the answer. Because Ms. Blakely was the only one who could make Darcy's dream come true.

Chapter Eight

After Darcy made her request that afternoon, Ruth Ann fought with herself all night and half of the next day. She'd never had trouble abiding by the rules at Hawkridge—with a schoolteacher for a mom, she knew the value of compliance.

And her last encounter with Jonah didn't encourage her to invite him back. She'd lost too many hours of sleep as it was, remembering those kisses, imagining others. Seeing him again would add fuel to a fire she couldn't seem to smother.

But he wanted to see Darcy take a riding lesson. He cared about his stepdaughter, wanted her to succeed. Ruth Ann knew she shouldn't even consider bending the school rules to relieve one parent's anxiety. If the parent were anyone else, she would simply say no and that would be the end.

Saying no to Jonah took more strength than she seemed to have, at least where Darcy was concerned. He wanted to be a good dad. How could she deny him the opportunity?

And Darcy had said, as she talked to Ruth Ann about the lesson, "I wish Jonah could watch. He always encourages me to do fun stuff, not just sit around and read. I bet he'd like seeing me ride."

Ruth Ann didn't have it in her to disappoint both of them.

So she sat down on the side of her bed that night with one of the business cards Jonah had left on the library conference table. His office number had a New York area code, not very helpful. The second number had been lined through, leaving only his cell phone number, which she dialed.

He picked up on the second ring. "Jonah Granger."

"Um…hi. It's Ruth Ann." When he didn't reply, she clarified. "Ruth Ann Blakely. From The Hawkridge School."

"I recognized you at 'Um,'" he said, in a laugh-warmed voice. "I was just shocked speechless to hear from you. What's going on? Is Darcy okay?"

"She's fine." Sinking back against her bed pillows, Ruth Ann let go of the breath she'd been holding. "I'm calling to break a rule."

Jonah chuckled. "I'm all in favor of rule-breaking. Which one are you going for?"

Did she imagine the wicked edge to his words? "The rule about no parent contact with students before Thanksgiving."

"Oh, that one." She definitely didn't imagine the disappointment in his tone. "I was hoping for something really exciting, but go on."

"Darcy wants to take a riding lesson. And she'd like you to be there."

"That's terrific. When should I show up?"

"How does tomorrow sound?"

A flat silence followed her question. "I'm going to Atlanta tomorrow morning," he said, at last. "I've got meetings scheduled on the building there from ten until six."

"That's too bad." Ruth Ann struggled to keep her voice unaffected by the huge lump of dismay lodged in her chest. "Darcy will be disappointed. But I suspect the excitement of being on horseback will compensate."

"How often is she taking lessons? I'll put the next one in my calendar, if you give me the date."

"I'm not setting up a full schedule yet—I don't want her to feel any pressure. Let's just see how the first one goes, and then she can tell me when she wants to do it again."

"Sounds good. Which horse are you going to put her on?"

"Dusty's a good beginner ride. You probably don't remember him—"

"Palomino, right? Third or fourth stall down? You said he likes peppermints. I'll be sure to get him a whole bag if he treats Darcy right."

"Oh, he will." Jonah remembered the horses. The knowledge scared her. "His favorite gait is stop."

"That should be safe enough."

A pause fell between them while she tried to think of something else to say. Really, though, they didn't have that much to talk about. "Okay, I'll be sure to let you know when Darcy takes another lesson. Have a good trip to Atlanta."

"I appreciate the call, Ruth Ann. Thanks for breaking the rule. Who knows? Maybe you can come up with some other rules that need breaking, if you put your mind to it." Without saying goodbye, he disconnected.

Ruth Ann lay sleepless for an extra hour that night, wondering exactly what kind of rules Jonah wanted her to break.

AFTER TWELVE HOURS of solving problems large and small with the Atlanta project, Jonah sat down on the bed in his hotel room, a tall glass of iced Scotch in one hand. With the other, he pressed an autodial number on his cell phone.

"Hello?"

"Hi." Surely she knew his voice by now. But then she didn't say anything else, and he wondered if he'd assumed too much. "Jonah Granger," he explained. "The architect."

"I know, I know," she said in an exasperated tone. "I recognized your voice, too."

He smiled to himself. "I thought I'd find out how Darcy's lesson went."

"We took everything slowly," Ruth Ann reported, her voice returning to its usual easy southern drawl. He'd given her something safe to talk about, and the tension between them immediately diffused. What about him did she find so threatening?

"Darcy brushed Dusty," she told him, "cleaned his hooves, put on the saddle and bridle with no problem."

"She's been around horses since before she started school." Jonah took a long draw on his drink. "I don't think she's ever been afraid of them on the ground."

"Right. So then we went out to the mounting block. Darcy started getting a little nervous. I guess the thoroughbred she rode last didn't stand well to be mounted."

"I don't really know. I guess I should have been there more often."

"Anyway, Dusty isn't that kind of horse. He stands quietly until you ask him to move. He's also not too tall—and I gathered the thoroughbred was huge. So, after some deep breathing, Darcy climbed up on the block, held on tight to the reins and the saddle, then threw her leg over and sat down."

"Way to go, Darcy!" Jonah pumped his arm in the air, splashing himself with Scotch and water in the process.

"Exactly." Ruth Ann's grin came through their wireless connection. "She just sat there for a while, getting the feel of a horse underneath her again. I think Dusty actually fell asleep for a few minutes."

She went on to tell him how she walked beside Dusty's head, fingers on the bridle, while Darcy first gripped the saddle, and then was able to hold just the reins. Before they finished, Darcy and Dusty had walked by themselves around the arena, as Darcy continued to relax.

"She came back to the center, dismounted and led him back to the barn, then untacked, gave him dinner and took him out to the pasture." Ruth Ann sighed. "The whole time, her face just glowed. She was so thrilled to be riding again. And I was thrilled for her."

"Terrific. Did she ask about another lesson?"

"She most certainly did. I suggested Monday afternoon."

"Damn."

"You'll be out of town again?"

"Charlotte. See, this is why I didn't know everything that was going on. Brittany kept me in the dark, and arranged for Darcy to be out of the way when I did get home."

Ruth Ann didn't say anything for a moment. "That's over, right? You're taking care of Darcy now, and your ex-wife is out of the way. Without her mother around, I suspect Darcy won't have as much trouble with depression. Especially once she gets comfortable on the back of a horse."

"I hope you're right." He relaxed back against the pillow. "So, have you broken any rules lately?"

She chuckled. "Does driving ten miles over the speed limit count?"

"It's a start."

"That's all I can think of. I mean, my life doesn't have that many rules to begin with."

"I'm not so sure. How about the rule that says men from the big city are all predators?"

"I—I didn't know there was a rule like that."

"You behave as if there were."

"I do not!"

"Or the rule that says beautiful women only come in sizes eight and under?"

"I didn't make that one."

"But you believe it exists, don't you?"

Ruth Ann sighed. "It's late, and I'm tired after working in the cold all day. I don't want to argue."

"I'll let you go and get some rest." He hesitated, then kept his voice low as he asked, "What about the rule that says you're supposed to sleep alone until after the wedding? Have you ever thought about breaking that one?"

The silence lasted so long, he began to wonder if they'd lost the connection. He looked at his phone, to be sure he still had power remaining. "Ruth Ann?"

"Not until recently," she said quietly. This time it was she who hung up without saying goodbye.

Jonah snapped his phone shut, polished off his drink, and went to sleep with a huge grin on his face.

RUTH ANN didn't know what to think when ten o'clock came and went on Friday night and the phone didn't ring. Then she tried to avoid thinking altogether by going to bed.

But all she could do was lie in the dark and wonder where he was and why he hadn't called again. Maybe he really had called last night to find out about Darcy and the rest of the conversation was simply a way to pass the time. He probably flirted with every woman who crossed his path. No doubt his questions about "the rules" were designed to give the poor deluded horse trainer a once-in-a-lifetime thrill.

Ruth Ann despised herself for playing right into his hands.

She'd told the students who came for lessons during the week that if they wanted to ride on the weekend they should do it Saturday, because the barn would be closed Sunday. Two of the school's maintenance workers were coming over to help repair the termite-damaged wall. Ruth Ann had finished digging out the floor herself, but had waited to replace the soil until the walls could be patched.

So when Saturday turned out to be gorgeous, with bright sunlight on the Technicolor tree leaves and a light, crisp breeze, many of her girls chose to spend an hour or two with the horses. Darcy came with Ingrid and set to work cleaning stalls, starting with Dusty's, of course. Ruth Ann asked if she wanted to ride, but the girl declined.

"I'm still sore from Thursday," she said, grinning. "Walking up the steps is agony! So I'll stretch out my muscles today and then be ready for a lesson on Monday."

Ruth Ann rode Waldo twice, taking two different sets of horses and their riders along the bridle paths winding through the woods. Howard Ridgely, with her great-granddad's help, had laid out five miles of trails across the mountainside. As carefully designed as today's ski slopes, the rides featured places to walk and trot, wider open spaces to canter, and even some sturdily built jumps for the adventurous. Waldo loved to jump, and Ruth Ann indulged him several times, so they both came back to the barn feeling successful and energized.

About four o'clock, as she supervised what would be the last riders of the day in the dressage arena and on the jumping course, Ruth Ann glanced toward the pasture, where Waldo and the other grays were grazing, and noticed an unfamiliar figure crouched by the fence. On the other side stood Snowflake, the miniature horse, presenting her tail to be scratched.

Ruth Ann made her way over to the fence. "That's a sign of high honor, if Snowflake allows you to scratch her rear end."

Eve didn't look up. "She likes it a lot."

"She does. And I get the feeling you've done this for her before."

Darcy's roommate shrugged one shoulder. "I come by sometimes on my runs."

"You're always welcome." Even wearing a sweatshirt and a down vest, Eve looked pitifully thin, her hands bony as she petted the horse, her cheekbones too sharp. Ruth Ann could guess where Darcy had gotten the idea of purging. "If you ever want to ride, let me know."

"Nah. All the other ones are too big. This is the only one I like." Keeping her eyes on Snowflake, Eve hadn't yet glanced in Ruth Ann's direction.

"She's a sweetie. You two have fun." Ruth Ann walked back toward the riding arenas. When she looked over a few minutes later, Eve was gone and Snowflake had wandered back to keep her buddy Waldo company.

The perfect fall day ended as every day did, with the feeding and transfer of horses from stall to field and back. After checking each stall latch and water bucket, Ruth Ann walked through the trees toward her blue cottage and a dinner of leftovers.

Saturday night loomed before her, and none of her standard activities seemed like an appealing way to fill the time. She could go into town for a movie—Ridgeville did possess a theater with two wide screens which showed the latest releases only a month or so after the rest of the country had seen them. Ruth Ann checked the newspaper, and decided she wouldn't enjoy a film filled with bathroom humor aimed at adolescent males nor a film filled with gory violence aimed at adolescent males. Besides, what if she went out and the phone rang?

Her answering machine would catch any calls, of course,

though it had been spectacularly useless for the last two days. No messages, no missed calls. Just…emptiness.

She put in a load of laundry, scanned the television schedule, which offered nothing of interest, and settled down with the book she'd been reading earlier in the week—a romance, with some pretty graphic love scenes that couldn't hold her attention. Where love scenes were concerned, her memories of those few minutes in Jonah's arms were more exciting than any imaginary hero and heroine could be.

After only a page or two, she gave up on the book and settled down to surf the Internet on her computer, looking at horses for sale, barn-supply sites, and job openings for horse trainers. The news there was bad enough to send her to the kitchen for a glass of wine.

When the phone rang, she thought for a second she'd imagined the sound. With her heart pounding, she waited until the third ring before picking up.

"I know it's late and you go to bed early," Jonah said, before she even managed a greeting. "I just got in from the airport and two days of hell in New York. Will you talk to me anyway?"

She went to curl up in the corner of her couch. "You were in New York?"

"Had to fly there from Atlanta. My partner was throwing a major tantrum and needed to vent face-to-face. Stephen is brilliant, but he does have the 'artistic temperament.'"

"So you run the practical side of the business?"

"Scary thought, isn't it?"

She grinned. "Terrifying."

"What's going on in the wonderful world of horses?"

Ruth Ann told him about Darcy showing up to work but not ride.

"Darcy works in the barn? Doing what?"

"Cleaning stalls, buckets, carrying hay, fetching horses—whatever needs to be done."

"Wow. I've never seen her do actual work. Or real physical activity of any kind, except for riding. Brittany's servants take care of…well, just about everything. Darcy grew up never having to lift a finger."

"She's lifting them now."

"Impressive. That's going to help her with her weight, I suspect."

"Definitely." Then she mentioned that Eve had been caught petting Snowflake. "I'm thinking—if she doesn't want to ride, maybe she would like to drive Snowflake."

"You mean in front of a cart?"

"We have a cute little carriage and the harness that fits Snowflake. I've never bothered—I'd look like Gulliver among the Lilliputians if I tried to drive that thing. But Eve's tiny, and she'd fit perfectly."

"Sounds like a possibility. I have a feeling Eve could use your peculiar brand of common-sense comfort."

A combination of embarrassment and pleasure left Ruth Ann speechless.

"Do you think Darcy might ride tomorrow?" Jonah asked. "I could come out to watch."

She hated to say no. "The barn will be closed tomorrow while a couple of guys from maintenance help me repair the termite damage in that end stall."

"Ah." Jonah didn't say anything for a minute. "Monday I'm leaving town again. You can let me know when her next lesson is scheduled, right? I'll be in Charlotte until Wednesday, but if she rode Thursday afternoon, I could show up. I'll drive my truck, so the powers that be don't immediately recognize they have a parent visiting."

The laugh in his voice inspired her own. "Good plan."

"And what's the latest broken rule?"

She couldn't think of one. "I…um…oh—I didn't have any vegetables at dinner. Just mashed potatoes and meatloaf."

"Not bad, not bad. At this rate, you'll find yourself doing something really wicked in no time at all. 'Night, Ruth Ann."

Jonah hung up the phone and let his body slide down against the pillows of his new bed. He'd told Ruth Ann the truth—the days in New York had been hell. Between the frantic pace of the city, the constant traffic noise, even in the middle of the night, and the concrete walls looming in every direction, he'd felt himself choking for lack of air and space. Stephen's usual hysterics left him tired and irritable, rather than just amused, as they once had. Halfway through dinner Friday night at his favorite restaurant, Jonah had found himself longing for a takeout pizza in his own living room in Ridgeville.

And Ruth Ann there to share it with him.

Even the two-hour drive from the airport in Asheville to his own driveway had provided a measure of relief. He'd resisted calling Ruth Ann from the car because the winding roads demanded attention he'd rather devote to the conversation. But when he got in, he saw how late it was and knew she'd be going to bed, if she wasn't there already.

Which was a pleasant thought, actually—Ruth Ann lying on smooth sheets, her silky hair spread out on the pillow, her lips parted in an inviting smile and nothing hiding that voluptuous body of hers but a soft woolen blanket.

After pacing around the three stories of his house for half an hour, he'd allowed himself to call, vowing that if she sounded the least bit sleepy he'd say a simple hello and hang up fast.

But she'd sounded completely awake. Even better, she'd sounded pleased to hear from him.

And now he knew what he'd be doing with his Sunday. Just what he needed after a long week hunched over design tables and contract pages—a full day of manual labor spent with a hammer and nails. And Ruth Ann Blakely.

Jonah could hardly wait.

HECTOR and Ruben Delgado, who arrived on Sunday morning to help with the barn repair, turned out to be some of the maintenance department's less experienced workers. Hector was twenty, Ruth Ann discovered, and Ruben eighteen. They'd been in the United States for about six months and spoke only a few words of English.

Ruth Ann, fortunately, had taken upper-level Spanish classes in college and spent a semester in Barcelona, so the communication barrier wasn't insurmountable. Using gestures and descriptions, she began to explain what she wanted them to do.

Then a voice from the front of the stall said, "That's not going to work, you know."

She whipped around to see Jonah standing there, with a box of doughnuts in hand. Excitement warred with irritation. "What are you doing here?"

"I brought calories for warmth and energy. Not to mention an extra pair of hands."

"You aren't going to rebuild my walls."

He gave a patient sigh. "We've been through this before. I won last time, and I'll win this time, too. Besides, I'm the one who actually knows something about building, remember?"

"But—" He came over and flipped up the top of the pastry box, offering her a choice, then Hector and Ruben. With her mouth full of powdered sugar and lemon cream, Ruth Ann said, "Why won't my plan work?"

"Short answer—you have to distribute the weight properly. Don't ask for the long answer." He set the box of doughnuts on a bucket out in the aisle and returned to the stall.

She finished the doughnut and, for lack of another option, wiped her fingers on the back of her jeans. "Okay, tell me what to do and I'll explain to Hector and Ruben. I really don't think—"

Jonah held up a hand for silence. Then he turned to the two young men and began speaking in fluent, idiomatic Spanish too rapid for her to follow. In a minute he had them laughing. The three of them went to stare at the broken walls, hands in their pockets, backs to Ruth Ann as they discussed—without her—the process of reconstruction.

She fumed for a moment in silence before stomping over and breaking up the all-guy conference.

"This is not the way things happen here," she told them all, with her glare targeting Jonah's face. "This is my barn. I make all the decisions. You three cowboys can talk amongst yourselves till the cows come home, but nothing gets done unless I say so." She crossed her arms over her chest. "So, what are you planning that I should know about?"

Jonah looked at the other two and shrugged. They shrugged in response. "They're from Costa Rica. We've been to a few of the same bars. My parents spent time there on research, and I know a couple of people at the embassy. I was just telling them I had some contacts if they ran into any issues with their work status."

Ruth Ann stared at him through narrowed eyes. "You're lying, just to make me feel foolish."

Jonah's blue gaze laughed at her. "Would I do that?"

"In a heartbeat," she told him. "So, what's your expert opinion on how to fix these walls?"

Chapter Nine

The four of them didn't get the job completed before the end of the day, but the most important structural issues had been dealt with. The rest, Jonah said, was cosmetic. Hector and Ruben could finish easily by themselves.

"Or," he told Ruth Ann, "you can manage alone. I wouldn't want to infringe on your status as barn boss. Stable maven. Whatever title you prefer."

"A simple 'ma'am' will do." She was washing out the coffee cups they'd used. Drying her hands on a paper towel, she turned and faced him. "I expect you to send me a bill for your work today, Jonah. This was a professional consultation."

"Yeah, right." They hadn't turned on the lights in the lounge, and the shadows of dusk obscured his face. "Do you want it on the official company letterhead?"

"Of course. You could add a line item for language tutoring. My Spanish improved quite a bit this afternoon."

"I'm not credentialed in education." He crossed the floor to stand in front of her. "Consider it a gift."

Taking the paper towel out of her grasp, he tossed it at the trash can and watch it float in. Then he touched his upturned fingertips to hers and lifted her hands between their bodies.

"Such hardworking hands," he said, gazing intently at them.

"Not exactly lily-white," Ruth Ann said, breathing fast. "Or silky-soft."

He shook his head. "No. But a capable woman must have capable hands."

Her breath deserted her completely when his hands eased around to hold hers and bring them up to rest against his cheeks. "Not silky, but not too rough. Warm." His palms slipped to her shoulders, but Ruth Ann held hers where he'd placed them, on the planes of his face, feeling his voice through his bones and flesh.

His eyes sparked in the darkness. "Want to break another rule?"

"Which one?"

He pulled her closer. "I'm sure there's a Hawkridge rule against teachers kissing parents. What do you think?"

"If there isn't," Ruth Ann said, "there should be."

No element of surprise, this time, no anger. And still the most amazing explosion of sensation in her chest, her knees, her toes. Jonah bent her slightly backwards against the counter, pressing his body into hers, and Ruth Ann sighed deep in her throat at the way they fit together.

And, oh, his mouth…delighting her with slow, sensuous kisses, demanding and giving at the same time. Needing to get closer, needing *more,* Ruth Ann curled her arms around Jonah's neck and opened herself to whatever thrill would come next.

"Sweet," Jonah muttered at some point. "So sweet. I've wanted this since I saw you with sugar all over your lips this morning."

The play of his teeth on her lower lip, the slide of his tongue across hers, the sweep of his hands from shoulders to hips so he could pull her even tighter against him… Ruth Ann savored each caress, tried to please him with her response and thought, from his reactions, that she succeeded.

But then, with his hands on her ribs and his knee between hers, he broke away to bury his face on her shoulder.

"Whoa," he said, after a moment. "Time to slow down."

Breathing hard, Ruth Ann squeezed her eyes shut, then opened them again. She thought about asking why, but wasn't sure she wanted to know the answer.

"Can't break all the rules at once," Jonah said, lifting his head and stepping back. "That's a sure way to get in trouble."

She gazed at him, still confused, still wanting. He smiled, and touched her cheek with his fingertips.

"It's killing me, but I'm going home now. See you Thursday for Darcy's lesson." One finger grazed her lips, the lower, then the upper. He hesitated.

Then, shaking his head, he walked to the exit, stepped out and closed the door quietly behind him. Ruth Ann heard his truck engine growl, the sound of wheels on gravel and pavement fading into silence.

She didn't understand why Jonah had stopped. Most guys wouldn't have, not with the barn empty all around them and a couch ten feet away. Surely Jonah had known he could take anything he wanted. Maybe he thought he was being fair, leaving her a choice in the decision of whether or not they had sex.

Or maybe he'd realized he simply didn't want her enough to stay.

And yet, he called again Monday night, from Charlotte. They talked briefly about Darcy's lesson, and then about football, elections and North Carolina barbecue, which he'd just tried for the first time. "I like the vinegar-based sauce," Jonah told her. "Not so gooey."

"Next you'll be telling me you like grits," she teased.

"I'd rather eat wallpaper paste."

On Tuesday, Darcy didn't come up at all during the conversation, but somehow they found enough to say that it was eleven-thirty before Ruth Ann checked her bedside clock. Wednesday's talk ended earlier, because she yawned in his ear.

"I'm sorry!" How could she have been so rude? "I'm not bored, honest."

"I kept you up too late last night, that's all. But I'll be there for Darcy's lesson tomorrow, so tonight I'll let you get some sleep. Broken any good rules lately?"

Ruth Ann sighed to herself. Only the one about not falling for a man you couldn't hold. "Nope. I'm staying on the straight and narrow this week."

"I'll have to see what I can do about that," he murmured. "Sweet dreams."

To Ruth Ann's amazement, her dreams that night were very sweet, indeed.

JAYNE THOMAS sat down beside Ruth Ann at breakfast in the dining hall Thursday morning. "We haven't seen you here for a while. Been sleeping in?"

"Staying up too late." Ruth Ann took a long sip of coffee, trying to wake herself up for the day after a restless night. "And the sun comes up so late in the fall, it's always hard for me to get up early."

"There's this useful invention called an alarm clock—"

"Yes, I know. I throw it across the room every morning."

They grinned at each other and finished their breakfasts while chatting about school business. As they walked their trays toward the dishwashing line, Jayne spoke over her shoulder.

"I heard something interesting about our architect yesterday."

Ruth Ann's heart slammed against the wall of her chest. "What would that be?"

"He's bought a house in Ridgeville."

"A house?"

"The Myers place. You know, that old Victorian out on Orchard Road?"

"Sure." Mrs. Myers had been friends with Ruth Ann's grandmother. Her daughter had gone to school with Ruth Ann's mom. "Why would Jonah Granger buy a house here?"

"I haven't had a chance to ask him. He's had lots of furniture delivered, according to Gina at the post office. Maybe he plans to spend school vacations here with Darcy."

"Maybe."

"Or he could be doing that thing—what's the word? Flipping? He could be flipping the house. Fixing it up and then selling it for a profit."

"You never know." Ruth Ann dumped her trash and set her tray on the conveyer belt. "Gotta get to work. See you later."

"But you would think," she told Waldo a short time later as she walked him to the pasture, "you would think he might have mentioned that he'd bought a house, sometime during the hours we've spent talking the last couple of weeks. An, 'Oh, by the way, I picked up a deal on a house last week,' might have been nice. Or, 'Hey, we're almost neighbors. I bought a rundown Victorian house for the hell of it.'"

She opened the gate and watched Waldo gallop into the open field, shaking out the stiffness from the night spent in a stall. "But, no, not a word. And what does that mean?"

Snowflake came outside next. "It means," Ruth Ann told her, "that I'm not the sun in his solar system. I'm, like, a moon on the far side of Jupiter. Interesting, maybe, but not terribly relevant." Snowflake trotted up to Waldo, and the two horses carefully checked out each others' scents before settling into the day's business of cropping grass.

"So all I have to do, Lainey, is back off fast." The oldest thoroughbred was the last of the grays to leave her stall this morning. "I might be able to salvage my pride, at least, if I don't let on how close I came to giving him anything he asked for. Remember what Mom always said." She leaned on the fence, watching Porcelaine claim her place in the herd. "Why buy the cow when you've been getting the milk for free?"

Resting her forehead on her crossed arms, Ruth Ann sighed. "Why does Mom always get to be right?"

THURSDAY AFTERNOON, Darcy was tying the laces on her paddock boots when Eve came into their room and fell face down on the bed. After a couple of minutes, she rolled over and opened her eyes.

"You're going to the stable again? Don't you get tired of nothing but work?"

"It's pretty fun, most days. Lots of girls are there, making jokes and stuff. Ms. Blakely is always kidding around. We have a good time. Plus, I'm taking lessons now, not just working." Standing at the mirror, Darcy pulled her hair back in a ponytail. "You could come."

Eve groaned. "Like I want to shovel horse poop all afternoon. I'm not even going running today. I feel like I got run over by a semi-trailer." She pushed her books and papers onto the floor, dragged the blanket up to her shoulders and yawned. "Don't let me sleep through dinner."

"Why not? You'll just throw it up if you eat it." Eve rolled over to face the wall. Regretting her meanness, Darcy gentled her voice. "You know the purging's really bad for you, Eve. It's making you sick and weak."

"It's keeping me thin."

"Nobody here cares if you're thin or not."

"I care."

"Why? It's not like there are any boys around, anyway."

"Boys aren't the issue."

"Your mom isn't here, either." Eve only burrowed deeper into the pillow. Darcy shrugged. "If you change your mind, you wouldn't have to start out cleaning stalls. There's other stuff to do. Or you could just watch a lesson, hang out at the fence with Snowflake. Did you know they have a little cart for him? You can drive him instead of riding. I bet that's almost as fun."

Again, no answer. Pulling on a sweatshirt, Darcy went to the door and flipped off the lights. "I'll get you up for dinner," she promised, and left the room.

Once at the barn, she didn't have to ask for directions on what she should do. She knew the routine now. Dusty waited for her in his stall, and was glad to munch on the carrots she'd brought him from the salad at lunch. When she'd been riding her mother's horses, she'd never had to brush or saddle them. The stable's grooms tacked up the horses and all she had to do was get on.

Now she knew the prep work was part of the fun. Dusty liked being brushed. He didn't mind having her pick up his hooves to clean them. She talked to him the whole time—just silly talk, like you might use with a child or a baby, telling him how pretty he was and how glad she was to be riding him. Darcy knew where his saddle and bridle were kept, and she was pretty sure she knew how to put them on. Ms. Blakely would double-check to be safe.

Darcy couldn't get over how good it could be to have someone like Ms. Blakely to count on. All the teachers at Hawkridge made her feel cared about. But Ms. Blakely made her feel loved. Almost like a sister. Or even a mom.

As she stood with Dusty in the stable yard, Ms. Blakely came out the back door of the barn.

"There you are," she said. "Right on time. Good job! Let's get started."

Darcy took a closer look at Ms. Blakely's face. She might have a cold—her eyes looked a little red, and her cheeks weren't as pink as usual. Her voice was definitely husky, as if her throat hurt.

"We don't have to have a lesson," Darcy volunteered. "I could just get on and ride him around the arena a few times. If you're not feeling good, I mean."

Ms. Blakely put her hands on her hips. "You're not getting out of work that easily! I'm fine. Let's get you mounted so we can begin."

Even though she knew Dusty would stand perfectly still for her to swing into the saddle, Darcy still felt nervous as she stood on the mounting block. If he moved while she only had one foot in a stirrup, she'd fall off. He might step on her, even step on her broken arm. That would hurt so bad….

"Darcy." Ms. Blakely stood at Dusty's head, a hand on his nose. "You're thinking too much. This horse is not going anywhere until you're settled in the saddle. Take a deep breath, blow it out. Another one. Now, grab his mane with your left hand and hold onto the saddle with your right. Left foot goes in the stirrup, and then just swing your leg over. That's right— don't drop your weight all at once. Use your leg muscles and ease down. Good. Now breathe again."

Darcy saw Ms. Blakely's grin and managed to breathe and smile back. With both feet in the stirrups, she wiggled her butt a little, getting comfortable. Then, with another deep breath, she picked up the reins, one in each hand.

"All set?"

She nodded in answer.

"So let's walk from here to the arena. Press your heels into Dusty's side and say 'Walk on.' Like you mean it."

"Dusty," Darcy said, looking ahead to where they were going, "Walk on."

JONAH intentionally arrived a few minutes after the start of Darcy's lesson. He didn't want to distract her, didn't want her thinking about him instead of herself and the horse.

So he stood within the shadows of the barn, leaning against the wall and watching from a distance as Ruth Ann conducted the lesson. Her instructions carried clearly through the chilly afternoon air. Darcy listened intently and seemed to follow directions quite well, at the walk, anyway.

About thirty minutes into the session, Ruth Ann upped the stakes. "Okay, Darcy, when you get to the top of the circle this time, I want you to press your heels into Dusty's side, a little harder than before, and say, 'Trot' in a nice, lively voice."

All motion in the arena stopped. After a minute, Darcy said, in a small voice, "Do I have to?"

Ruth Ann answered immediately, "Yes."

Inside the barn, Jonah straightened up. Darcy did not have to trot if she didn't want to. This was only her third lesson, for God's sake.

"I don't want to trot," Darcy said.

Jonah nodded to himself. Good for her.

"I know that," Ruth Ann replied. "But I'm the teacher, and I want you to trot."

Darcy sat with her hands on the saddle in front of her and her chin down, her lower lip stuck out in a pout. "No."

Ruth Ann stood calm and relaxed in the center of the circle Darcy had been riding. "Because you're afraid?"

Darcy nodded.

"Well, you have two choices." She held out her left hand, palm up. "You can choose to do as I've asked and trot the horse." Her right hand came out. "Or you can dismount, put the horse away, and find some other place to spend your afternoons."

Darcy jerked her head up. "You mean you wouldn't let me come back to the barn? Just because I don't want to trot?"

Jonah started for the arena. No way was he letting Ruth Ann treat his stepdaughter with such blatant disregard for her feelings and the trauma she'd endured.

Ruth Ann crossed her arms over her chest. "Either you trust me, Darcy, or you don't."

Jonah stopped in his tracks.

"Either you believe I'm taking care of you, that I won't ask you to do anything I don't know is completely within your power, or you don't. And if you don't trust me, then there's no point in continuing these lessons. You might as well find something else you enjoying doing, because we can't work together."

"Oh," Darcy said. After a couple of minutes, she took a deep breath and straightened her back. Dusty started to walk again, following a circle with Ruth Ann as its center.

"That's right," she said, "keep your heels down. Hands down, too. Now, as you come up to the top, squeeze your heels together. Shorten your reins and say the *T*-word."

"Trot," Darcy whispered. Dusty paid no attention, and kept on walking.

"He's got to hear you, Darcy." Ruth Ann laughed. "Put some guts into it, girl."

As Dusty came back toward the crucial point, Jonah saw Darcy preparing herself. He could have sworn he heard her deep breath. And then she said, "Trot! Trot, Dusty!"

Dusty pricked his ears, swished his tail, and moved into a slow, steady trot.

"Way to go," Jonah yelled, clapping his hands and striding out toward the arena. "Excellent!"

His shout drew Darcy's attention. She jerked her head around and saw him. "Jonah?"

Dusty continued his trot. But Darcy had stopped thinking and started wobbling. In the next instant, she leaned to the inside…and lost contact with the saddle altogether.

Ruth Ann flashed one searing glance in Jonah's direction. "Get the horse," she told him. Then she went to kneel in the dirt by Darcy's side.

"You okay, baby? Everything still attached?"

Dusty had wandered all of about twenty feet past where Darcy fell. Jonah picked up the reins and drew the horse along behind him as he approached. "Darcy, I'm so sorry. Are you all right?"

Darcy sat up, spitting out dirt. "I told you," she said. "I always fall." Ruth Ann brushed off her back and arms and head. "I can't believe how stupid that was." She made a motion to get up, and Ruth Ann reached out an arm to help her.

But Darcy pushed her off. "I'll do it myself." Putting her hands flat on the ground, she moved onto her knees and then, from all fours, pushed herself to her feet.

Dusting her rear end, she glared at Jonah. "At least this time, I know it wasn't my fault. Why did you yell at me in the middle of a lesson?"

He actually took a step back, he was so startled. "I was celebrating your trot. I did say I was sorry."

Darcy rolled her eyes. "I'm glad you're here. But stay quiet, please. I need to concentrate." She looked at Ruth Ann. "Can I try again?"

Jonah said, "Don't you think you've done enough for one day?"

The two females turned their heads to stare at him. Their

identical expressions asked, *Are you crazy?* Then they looked at each other again.

"You have to get back on," Ruth Ann told Darcy. "I'll give you a leg up."

Neither of them had a word for Jonah as Ruth Ann took Dusty's reins from him and walked the horse to the center of the riding area. Understanding he'd been dismissed, Jonah went to one of the benches along the side of the arena and sat down. There was more to this horse business than he could understand. But Ruth Ann and Darcy apparently knew everything he was missing.

The next episode of trot went better, because Jonah kept his mouth shut. Before the lesson ended, Darcy had trotted Dusty in a complete circle, clockwise and counterclockwise. By then, an audience of several girls had collected behind the bench on which Jonah sat. When Darcy finished, they gave her a round of applause.

"Yay, Darcy!"

"Way to go!"

"Good ride!"

Laughing and, as Ruth Ann had said, glowing, Darcy slid out of the saddle and walked her horse toward the barn. The girls surrounded her, a cadre of supporters.

"See," Ruth Ann said, walking up to the bench he sat on. "She's doing well at Hawkridge. She's found friends and something she really loves to keep her busy."

"That's terrific." Jonah got to his feet, noticing that the sun had dropped behind the trees. "I'd say we owe a lot of what she's accomplished to you. You're really good with her. I would have let her put off trotting until another time."

"I thought she might never work up the courage, if I let her get away with backing out today."

"And you were probably right. I wish she hadn't fallen, but at least she wasn't hurt."

"You have to expect the unexpected, even on a horse as quiet as Dusty. She finished her lesson, that's the important part."

"She couldn't have waited until next time?"

Ruth Ann shook her head. "Unless you're seriously injured, you get back on right away. Otherwise, you lose your nerve." She looked at him out of the sides of her eyes. "Haven't you ever fallen?"

"Off a horse? Never." Jonah used a finger to turn Ruth Ann's head so that her eyes met his. "I've had experience with bad rides of a different kind, though. I had pretty much convinced myself not to try again. The pain didn't seem worth the effort."

She didn't pretend to misunderstand him. "Does that mean you've changed your mind?"

"I'm considering the possibility," he confessed. "Considering it very seriously."

To his surprise, she didn't comment. Or even smile. Ruth Ann gazed at him for a moment, her gold-green eyes serious and, he decided, wary.

"What are you afraid of?" he asked on impulse. "Why do I make you so nervous?"

"I believed in Santa Claus," she said, "the Tooth Fairy and the Easter Bunny." Her shoulders lifted on a deep breath. "They weren't real, either. Goodnight, Jonah."

She walked into the barn and turned on the lights, leaving him standing outside, alone, in the dark.

Chapter Ten

The Hawkridge board meeting to consider the new stable proposal was a great success...because Ruth Ann Blakely didn't attend.

With five minutes to spare before the scheduled three o'clock start time, Jonah eased through the crowd to stand beside Jayne Thomas. "Where is she?"

The headmistress shrugged one shoulder. "She's probably running late, as usual." But Jayne's frown was a worried one.

She delayed the opening of the meeting five minutes, just in case. But then Miriam Edwards took a seat at the table and the rest of the board members followed suit. Confronted with expectant silence, Jayne had no choice but to begin.

Jonah gave the talk he'd prepared, citing Ruth Ann's comments and her tour of the existing stable as sources of assistance as well as inspiration. He explained the changes he'd made—lower ceilings, more functional spaces, more horse-friendly materials—but mentioned the upscale materials and amenities, as well. On every point, he met with approval and compliments. When he'd finished, the board members gave him a round of applause.

But Ruth Ann never showed up.

Even his cost estimate barely caused a ripple, primarily because Miriam Edwards would foot a significant portion of the bill. As coffee cups were refilled and the plate of cookies made another trip around the table, Jonah decided he might as well go for broke. Returning to the front of the room, he cleared his throat to get the crowd's attention.

"If we started construction tomorrow—and we can't, because the site has to be cleared—this stable would not be usable, let alone finished, until next October," he told them. "In the meantime, Hawkridge students must continue to use the existing barn."

He paused, making sure all eyes were on him. "But that existing structure needs some work. The roof leaks and there are termite problems. At the very minimum, these issues must be addressed. I also recommend an electrical inspection. Before you vote funds for the new facility, I strongly urge you to make money available to Ms. Blakely for the upgrades the old stable desperately needs."

After a moment of silence, an ugly squabble erupted across the conference table. Miriam didn't want to throw good money at a hopeless situation. Her supporters and opponents squared off, assaulting their adversaries with words like *parsimonious* and *miserly, improvident* and *spendthrift*.

The headmistress joined Jonah at the front of the room. "You should have run this idea by me first," she told him in a low voice. "I could have prepared you for this reaction. Ruth Ann and her father have always managed with far less funding than they needed. That's why I wanted her to agree to the new barn—her cooperation would increase the flow of money in her direction." Jayne sighed. "Of course, this 'discussion' would be much more violent if Ruth Ann were here."

"Oh, I don't know." Jonah gave a short laugh. "At the first

sign of resistance, I think she would have told them all to go to hell and walked out."

Jayne smiled. "You might be right."

In the end, the board voted to pay for a termite inspection and basic repairs to all the affected walls, using the school's maintenance crew for labor. The electrical inspection was tabled until after the new year, as were roof repairs.

Listening to the board members bicker, Jonah seriously contemplated withdrawing from the barn project altogether. Their stinginess frustrated and disgusted him. He could make his plan contingent on repairs to Ruth Ann's barn—maybe that would spur them to behave with decency. Or else…

Or else, he realized, Miriam would take offense and withdraw her money altogether. Then there would be no new barn and no repairs at all to the old one. Even Ruth Ann would not be satisfied in that case, because the termite damage had been revealed.

And he would lose the capital he needed to establish his business in Ridgeville, where he now owned a house.

So Jonah kept quiet. By the time the room had emptied of everyone but himself and Jayne Thomas, however, his enthusiasm for the project had vanished.

"Don't look so glum," Jayne told him, gathering coffee cups onto a tray. "This is just the way boards work. If they threw their money at everyone who asked for it, they'd run out very quickly. And then where would we all be?"

"Making do, I guess. The way Ruth Ann always has." He eased his drawings back into their box. "I'm going to drive over there and—"

"Check on her? Confront her?" Jayne shook her head. "Try not to argue. She's not nearly as resilient as she seems to be. Or…" she said, more to herself than him, "…believes she is."

Keeping those words in mind, Jonah drove slowly along the back road toward the stable, allowing the cool breeze and golden slanted light of late afternoon to ease his mind. He would work out something to correct the problems in Ruth Ann's barn if he had to nail the shingles onto the damn roof himself.

Again today, the barn stood quiet and still, with no evidence of students or equines. Apparently, Ruth Ann hadn't used lessons as an excuse to miss the board meeting.

Then, in the silence, he heard the clop-clop of horse hooves on stone, moving toward the back of the barn. Shrugging into a jacket, Jonah headed in that direction to see what was going on.

He stopped at the corner of the building, just out of sight. In the cobbled courtyard which led to the training arenas and pastures, Ruth Ann stood alone with Waldo. The giant gray horse wore a shiny black bridle decorated with silver and an equally polished black saddle over a scarlet pad. As Ruth Ann tightened the girth strap running underneath the horse's belly, Waldo stood with his head high, his ears pricked forward, his eyes bright and knowing. Clearly, he anticipated with pleasure whatever was about to happen.

Satisfied with the saddle, Ruth Ann pulled the stirrups into place, led Waldo to the mounting block and climbed onto his back. She wore her usual tan breeches, but today a white turtleneck had replaced the standard T-shirt. More surprising still, she'd donned a cutaway black jacket—only waist-length in front, but with two knee-length "tails" in back. Silver buttons adorned the coat's front panel and sleeve cuffs. Her ponytail had been twisted into a knot at the nape of her neck, and a black derby hat sat on her head. Tall black boots with a mirror-bright finish completed the outfit, which Jonah recognized as the basic uniform for upper-level dressage competition.

Then the music started, an old rock-and-roll tune designed to get the blood pumping. Jonah looked for the source of the sound and saw a big boom box sitting on the brick wall of the stable yard, no doubt operated by remote control. For almost half an hour, Ruth Ann rode Waldo to random selections of music at different speeds and in every direction, and Jonah realized this was just a warmup for the main event. He didn't think about moving, getting closer, making his presence known. If she realized he was there, she wouldn't finish what she'd started. And he couldn't wait to see what came next.

The music stopped abruptly, though Waldo and Ruth Ann continued trotting around the outside of the arena through several minutes of absolute silence. Jonah held his breath, waiting.

Without warning, the initial crashing chords of the theme from "Phantom of the Opera" shattered the peaceful afternoon. At that precise moment, Ruth Ann and Waldo entered the arena in a perfectly timed trot—with slow and stately grace, Waldo lifted his knees shoulder-high, hesitating at the top before switching legs. Neck curved in a majestic arch, every muscle and nerve focused on Ruth Ann's direction, the gray horse paraded to the center of the arena where, without missing a beat, he picked up a canter.

That was just the beginning of the magic. As the music moved, so did horse and rider, performing a dance which was by turns dramatic, lyrical and volatile. Ruth Ann hardly stirred in the saddle, yet she had to be telling the horse when to perform each separate movement.

Finally, Waldo came down the center line of the arena once again. The music swelled, then diminished, until only the tinkling notes of a music box could be heard. Waldo stopped in the exact middle of the space, bent one front leg back and bowed. Removing her hat with one hand, Ruth dropped her hand to her side and her chin to her chest. The two performers posed motionless for a silent moment.

Then the world fell back into place. Waldo straightened up, shaking his head and snorting. Ruth Ann leaned over to hug his neck. Jonah wiped the tears off his cheeks with a jacket sleeve before walking toward the arena to the sound of his own applause.

"Bravo," he yelled. "Bravo!"

Ruth Ann whipped her head around and saw him. "What the hell are you doing here?"

"Watching a masterful performance. It was brilliant. Astounding. I've never seen such an exhibition."

She shook her head, but she was smiling as she stroked Waldo's neck. "Oh, we made lots of mistakes, things you wouldn't see if you didn't know what to look for. But it's fun."

"He doesn't do shows anymore?" Jonah stopped beside Waldo's head and put a hand on the smooth cheek, then rubbed him under the chin.

"Too old." Ruth Ann slid out of the saddle and pulled the reins over Waldo's head. "We do this every few weeks because we enjoy it, but his back legs wouldn't stand up to daily training. He's an old man, that's all there is to it." She kissed Waldo's nose and began to lead him toward the barn.

Jonah followed, whether she wanted him to or not. "Do you ever demonstrate for your students? Show them what they can achieve?"

Ruth Ann shrugged. "We have lots of videos and disks of competitions. They're free to watch."

"That's not the same as seeing it in person." As she shed the jacket and the derby, Jonah held out his arm. "I'll take them."

Her eyes widened in surprise, but she handed him the coat

and hat. "I would think they'd rather ride themselves than watch a couple of has-beens like us strut their stuff."

"I believe Darcy would be completely mesmerized by what I've seen today. Not to mention inspired."

"She's pretty inspired already." Ruth Ann exchanged Waldo's bridle for a halter and removed his saddle. "She came Saturday and Sunday to clean stalls and ride."

"I still think you should show the students what you and Waldo can achieve."

Shaking her head, Ruth Ann brushed Waldo's neck, his shoulders and back. "I'm not going to call them all down and make them sit through a performance. That would be... weird." Turning her back, she bent down to brush Waldo's rear legs.

Jonah gave a silent groan and shut his eyes. Rounded hips, a firm bottom, shapely legs in tight-fitting breeches and tall boots...did she know what the sight of her did to a man? To *this* man?

"What's wrong?"

He opened his eyes to find her staring at him. "Nothing. Nothing at all. If you don't want to perform by yourself, have you thought about demonstrating on Waldo as part of a student show?"

"Some of the students compete in horse shows around the area. Is that what you mean? Because I don't thin—"

"No. I mean a show here. At Hawkridge." The idea was exploding in his head, fully formed.

Ruth Ann fetched a blanket to put over Waldo. "We've never done anything like that."

"But you could. Say, the weekend the parents come to get the girls before Thanksgiving."

"Why?"

"Why not? You could show off what your girls accomplish here. You could, in an understated way, solicit donations from parents to support the equestrian program. More girls might be attracted to riding when they see the results—your students doing their thing and then you and Waldo."

She pursed her lips as she gave it some thought. At the sight of her soft mouth imitating a kiss, the desire Jonah had been trying to ignore flared high. He shifted his stance, driving his hands into the pockets of his jeans.

"Five weeks isn't much time to put a show together," she said. But the spark in her eyes, the new energy in her movements, betrayed her excitement at the idea. "It could be fun, though. A goal for the girls to work toward."

"Exactly."

"I'd have to ask Jayne, of course. And she'd probably have to take it to the board." Ruth Ann frowned. "Miriam might try to sabotage me."

"Leave Miriam to me."

That was the wrong thing to say. "Oh, of course." Ruth Ann made a frustrated gesture. "You'll tell her how good it would be for the new stable. You'll probably promise her the donations that come in. Right, I should have remembered which side you're on." Unclipping Waldo's halter from ropes attached to rings in the wall, she led him down the aisle, toward his stall.

Jonah waited until the horse was safely inside and the door closed. Then he planted himself in the center of the aisle, preventing Ruth Ann from returning to the front of the barn. When she tried to step around him, he moved in the same direction, side to side, until she made a frustrated noise and stood still.

When he was sure she was listening, he said, "That is not what I meant, and if you looked past your own prejudice you'd know it."

"Prejudice?" Hands on her hips, she glared at him.

"You've been biased against me since before you ever set eyes on me."

"Not you, personally. Your project."

"You won't admit that I'm trying to work the situation out to everyone's benefit."

"You won't admit that simply isn't possible."

"Only because you won't try to compromise. Why didn't you come to the meeting today?"

She waved a hand, dismissing the idea. "I didn't want to waste the energy."

"I've completely revised the plan. You might find you like it now."

"That's irrelevant, isn't it?"

"Doesn't have to be. Jayne would prefer you stayed."

"Miriam has a different agenda." She smiled when he gave her a questioning look. "I've talked to other trainers and teachers in the area. She's got someone she wants to place at Hawkridge—a handsome young guy from Germany, I'm told. I played into her hands, getting so mad at that first presentation."

"And again today, by staying away. You could have gotten some of the board members on your side, if you'd been there."

"Jayne said something a couple of weeks ago that stayed with me." Ruth Ann turned back to Waldo's stall. "Life is about change. Sometimes you have to accept defeat and move on to a different place." As she checked the latch on the lower half of the door, she shrugged. "Maybe this is that time for me."

While Jonah absorbed the abrupt change in her attitude, Ruth Ann slipped by him and headed down the aisle. "I need to feed the horses," she said over her shoulder. "Have a good night."

Jonah understood he'd been dismissed. Too bad. "Why don't I show you the new design?"

She stopped but didn't turn around. "I don't see the point."

"So humor me." He jogged down the aisle to catch up with her. "You can tell me everything that's wrong with the plan. That should liven up your evening." When he looked over, he saw her mouth tilt in a one-sided smile. "See, you could have a great time giving me hell."

She bent over to pick up a tall stack of clean buckets. "And what would you get out of the experience?"

Jonah went for the easy answer. "Company for dinner. I'll drive into town and bring back a couple of pizzas. How's that?"

All he could see above the buckets were her eyes, which went round with surprise. "You want to eat in the barn?"

He shook his head. "The light's not too good, even in the lounge. How about your house?"

"My house?" Her voice squeaked on the second word.

"You live in one of the Hawkridge cottages, right? The blue one nearest the barn?"

The buckets went up and down as Ruth Ann nodded.

"Okay, then. You get your work done here. I'll head in for pizza, and we'll probably get back to your place at about the same time. Don't rush—if I'm there first, I'll save you a slice or two." He grinned to let her know he was kidding. "Anything you don't like on pizza?"

"Anchovies."

"But that's my favorite!" Then he realized she'd take him seriously, and shook his head. "No, it's not. I'll see you in an hour or so." As he passed her, he allowed himself to touch her, to cup the ball of her shoulder briefly, taking with him the smooth definition of muscle under her sleeve.

Insane, he told himself, driving away from the school. *Crazy.* He didn't bribe people to consider his designs. Since his first semester at Harvard, he'd been one of the stars—his projects were chosen for awards and articles in the yearbooks, he'd had his choice of summer internships. Before he'd finished the program, three commissions had landed on his desk.

Now he was begging someone to look at his work, someone who wouldn't be able to afford his hourly fee on the design of an outhouse. But he wanted Ruth Ann to approve.

He wanted her to approve of *him.*

This afternoon, watching her ride, he'd seen Ruth Ann without the defenses and evasions she used to protect herself. Her gentle control of the big animal she'd chosen as a partner had left Jonah in awe. Energy, intelligence, discipline and focus were the tools she used to deal with horses, as well as with lost girls like Darcy, blended with an immense compassion and capacity to care. He wanted those qualities to transform his own life.

If he hadn't known before today, he now recognized the truth. He'd fallen in love.

THE DOORBELL rang before Ruth Ann had figured out what to wear.

"Pizza man," Jonah called. "Expecting a substantial tip for keeping his fingers out of the boxes."

"Just a second," she yelled back. She couldn't very well go to the door in a bra and panties, even if they were the nicest ones she owned. Even if one of the fantasies she'd allowed herself about Jonah did begin that way…

"No." At the closet, she pulled out a pair of black velour pants and a gold, long-sleeved T-shirt. No time for socks, no shoes that worked—she'd have to go barefoot. Casual. Relaxed.

Opening the front door, she tried to get her breathing under control. "Hi. Come in. Sorry to keep you waiting."

But Jonah just stood there staring, as he balanced two pizza boxes on one hand and clutched a paper bag with the other. "Your hair—"

"What?" She put a hand to her head. "What's wrong with my hair?"

"Nothing." He shook his head, and finally came inside, just before her toes dropped off like chips of ice. "I so rarely see you without the ponytail. That's all."

"Oh." She'd brushed her hair, but forgotten to put it back up. "I'll be right ba—"

"No. Don't." He put out the hand holding the paper bag as a barrier. "It looks good. I like it."

Now she didn't know what to do. Or say. "Um…okay. Thanks. Again." She'd known this would be hard. "The dining room is over here. You can put the boxes on the table."

He set the bag down first, with clunk. "I picked up a bottle of Chianti. I thought that might taste good with pizza." Opening the boxes, he presented them with a gesture. "Pepperoni mushroom or sausage green pepper. Take your pick."

"I love sausage and pepper pizza." Ruth Ann eyed him with suspicion. "How did you know that?"

Jonah took the wine bottle out of the bag and began to peel away the seal. "I might have mentioned, as I was ordering, that you'd be sharing the pizza. And the guy taking my order might possibly have pointed out what you always asked for when you came in." He grinned at her. "Sounds good to me, too. Though I also got my own favorite, just to be safe." His hands twisted slightly on the neck of the bottle and the cork ejected with a gentle pop.

"I'll get glasses." In the kitchen, with the door closed between them, Ruth Ann took a moment to breathe. Pizza and wine…with Jonah Granger in her own house. It sounded almost romantic.

Except this wasn't romance, it was business. He wanted her to look at his design, give him feedback using her expertise as a trainer. Period. Yes, he'd said he liked her hair loose. He probably flattered Miriam Edwards the same way.

Did he call Miriam at night and suggest breaking the rules in that tempting voice? Had he kissed Miriam Edwards the way he kissed *her?*

The idea made Ruth Ann's blood boil, her stomach clench. Surely not. But then, he hadn't told *her* he'd bought a house in town. What the hell was she supposed to think?

"Are you hand-blowing those glasses?" Jonah asked from the dining room. "The pizza is getting cold."

"Coming." Using wineglasses would send the wrong signal, so she grabbed a couple of short, fat tumblers from the cabinet. Paper plates and plain paper napkins conveyed no expectations. Armed with neutral dinnerware, she returned to the dining room.

Jonah had taken off his leather jacket and now sat with his elbows propped on her dining-room table, waiting for her to return. He'd rolled up the sleeves of his blue-and-white pin-stripe dress shirt and released an extra button at the neck. His hair looked less styled than usual, but his mood seemed somber, more tense than when he'd left the barn. His eyes were still the most gorgeous blue she'd ever seen.

Her heart pounded like Waldo's hooves at a full gallop.

"Sorry to keep you waiting. You must be hungry." She set the glasses and paper products next to the pizza boxes. "Go ahead and eat."

As she took a chair, he pushed a tumbler in front of her and poured wine nearly to the brim. He filled his own glass only halfway up. At her questioning look, he said, "I have to drive home."

"Right." He wasn't pretending this was a date. That was a good thing. A good thing which made her feel lousy.

He glanced around them as they ate. "You're neat."

"Neat?"

"Not messy. Organized."

"Oh. Yeah, my mother didn't allow a messy room. I learned to pick up after myself pretty early. Plus, I'm not here that much—mostly just to sleep. I spend just about all day every day at the barn."

"Which you also keep very neat and as clean as could be expected."

She shrugged. "It's easier to work when everything's where it's supposed to be."

"I don't know." He leaned back in his chair, wiped his mouth with a paper napkin and then clasped his hands in front of his belt buckle. "I kind of like having the pieces all lying around—the pages I've drawn and discarded, the pencils and notes and rulers scattered everywhere. Sometimes I get stuck, and looking at the previous versions will bring back an idea I need. Or the process of trying to find the ruler will give me a break, and a solution will pop up when I'm thinking about something else."

"In other words, you're a slob?"

"More or less. I clean up, eventually. Then I start making the next mess."

"I'm glad I'm not your housekeeper." Which seemed to be a perfect opening for the question burning the tip of her tongue. "I…um…hear you bought a house in Ridgeville."

He took another sip of wine. "Yes, I did. An old Victorian on Orchard Lane."

She nodded. "The Myers place. I've been there. My mother was friends with Mrs. Myers's daughter."

"It's a great house." He brought his arms up to prop his elbows on the table. "Big rooms, all with fireplaces and lots of windows, great views of the mountains and fields. I think Darcy's really going to like living there."

"You bought it for Darcy?"

"Well, partly. I'll have my office there, as well. I'm moving my business from New York to North Carolina."

He said it so easily, as if she hadn't agonized over this issue since she'd seen him last week. "You…um…hadn't mentioned that before."

His eyes widened. "I guess not. It wasn't a secret—we just always seem to have something else to talk about. Where did you think I was staying?"

"I didn't think, I guess. The hotel, the b & b maybe…" She drew a deep breath to give her courage. "Why are you relocating?"

He twiddled his thumbs. "I told you about my temperamental partner." She nodded. "Well, that's the biggest reason. I'm tired of his dramatics. Plus, I wanted somewhere quiet, less frantic, than any of the big east-coast cities, including Atlanta. When I came to visit Hawkridge concerning the stable project, I thought these mountains were the most beautiful I'd ever seen. The first time I took a deep breath I felt…well, like I was home."

Ruth Ann sighed. "I know what you mean. I'm not sure I'll ever feel as comfortable anyplace else."

"Despite what you said in the barn, you don't have to. You can live your entire life right here."

"I don't think it's an issue we can settle tonight." She stood up and scooted her chair in. "So, how about those drawings you wanted me to look at? I'll move the pizza boxes and you can lay them out on the table. Will that be okay?"

"Sure."

Bustling around, getting rid of the trash and leftovers from the meal, Ruth Ann was very aware of Jonah's slower, easier movements. She wished she could relax. But she was afraid of betraying herself, afraid she'd reveal more about her feelings toward him than she wanted him to know. Than she wanted to know, herself.

And so she stood stiffly upright as she studied the drawings he laid on the table. The building itself was beautiful, modern and yet classic, with tall brick arches and elegant columns, plus high windows on all four walls to bring in light and air. Automatic water sources, ceiling fans and built-in hay mangers created palaces out of the horse stalls. At the same time, he'd simplified the lounge—the furniture was less elaborate than before and the appliances not quite so expensive. She could see he'd taken her comments seriously, arranging the tack and feed rooms and the wash stalls more conveniently.

"You made a lot of changes," she said carefully. "I can tell you've done some in-depth research."

"Right. And?" He crossed his arms over his chest, waiting.

"And it's…okay. I mean, some people might find this barn appealing."

"Some people did—the board of directors for The Hawkridge School approved the plan and the contract this afternoon."

"Well, there you go. You don't need anything from me."

He slapped his hands on the table, so hard that two drawings fell off. "Dammit, Ruth Ann, tell me what you think."

She took a deep breath. "As barns go, I've seen a lot worse. But I couldn't…I wouldn't like working there."

"Why not?"

Chapter Eleven

Ruth Ann sighed and rubbed her tired eyes with the fingers of one hand. She should have known he'd come back with that question.

He followed up with, "What's wrong with it?"

"Have you looked at a lot of barns, Jonah?" Dropping her hand to her side, she met his gaze. "How many working stables have you visited?"

"Fifteen, twenty. Not," he said in a biting tone, "including the one I built in Connecticut."

"Did they look like this design?"

"Some did. Most didn't. Most were just rows of stalls protected by an outer wall and a roof."

"If you visited enough working barns, you'd see that most of them are lines of stalls, as you put it, with a roof and an outside wall. Some people do construct very grand buildings for their horses. Those people generally also have the money to pay a large staff to do the work. Or, sometimes, they don't actually have enough horses to require much work."

"Keep going." He picked up his wine and walked into her living room to sit on the couch. "I'm listening."

Ruth Ann brought her own glass along and went to perch on the edge of the recliner.

"Here's what's really wrong—your design is being approved by people who will rarely use this barn. Miriam Edwards wants a show place for her German genius, but I wonder what *he* wants. Maybe he would like simple, clean lines, ceilings only as high as they need to be to keep a horse from hitting its head, plain corners and plenty of storage. Maybe he would like the windows where the horses could use them to look outside, get a cross-flow of fresh air while they're in the stalls."

"You're saying my barn is too elaborate?"

"For me. Maybe not for the German wonder boy. There are some very fancy stables in Germany, and some very plain ones. Really, your best bet would be to work with the person who will be using the barn—"

"That's what I'm trying to do." He frowned at her, one eyebrow raised. "But you keep avoiding me."

Somehow, while they'd talked, Jonah had moved to the end of the sofa nearest the recliner. He was sitting forward, now, his left knee almost touching her right at the corner of the coffee table. Like her, he held his wineglass with both hands, between his knees. That meant their hands were close, as well. And when she looked up from her own drink, his face was right *there.* She could see the dark flecks in the sky-blue of his eyes, the fine texture of his skin, the tiny wrinkles that made his mouth so soft, so agile when he kissed....

Ruth Ann cleared her throat and sat back in the recliner, pulling her bare feet up under her hip. "I've told you—I don't want a new barn. If I stay at Hawkridge, I want to use the barn I have. If you—they—insist on a new barn, then I won't be the one using it."

"We're talking in circles." He thunked his empty glass on the coffee table. "Why is it all or nothing with you? Either you keep your barn or you leave the school altogether. Is there no middle ground?"

"I—"

"Of course there isn't." Jonah stood up, shaking his head. "I knew that before I came." Back in the dining room, he gathered the drawings together so roughly that Ruth Ann could hear the papers brushing against each other. By the time she straightened up out of the recliner, he'd come back with his jacket on and the box of drawings under one arm, ready to leave.

"This isn't a personal issue," Ruth Ann began, because he was acting very much like a rejected lover. "I don't—"

"It damn sure is personal," he told her, almost snarling. "Because you have somehow wrapped your entire life around this one building. You're in control there. You think you're prepared to deal with surprises because there really aren't any—you've been in this one place so long, you've seen everything that might happen, so you know what to do in any given situation."

"You're implying that I'm scared?"

"Actually, I'll say it outright. You're scared, Ruth Ann. You're afraid to step beyond this fence you've built and find out what you don't know. My guess is that you don't think you can handle it, that you'll fail some test, fall short of somebody's standards. Well, you know what? That happens to everybody."

He knocked the knuckles of his free hand on the box of drawings. "Including me. You've told me twice now that I don't measure up."

From deep inside her, anger erupted. "You're not exactly Mr. Easy-to-Please, yourself."

"What are you talking about?"

"You came into the school looking down that arrogant nose at anybody who didn't fawn over you and immediately love your designs."

"Not at all." But his cheeks reddened.

"You didn't even look at my barn before you passed judgment on it. Not new enough, not big enough, not fancy enough—you didn't ask if it *worked,* if it suited the needs of the people who used it."

"I had been told—"

"Then you walked in and started criticizing. Too much beige and brown. Uneven floors. Rotten beams and walls—"

"You know that's a safety issue. The horses and the students are in danger if the structure is unsound."

"I know my barn and I are simply not good enough. Not good enough for Miriam Edwards, and not good enough for you."

"I never said that."

"You didn't have to—your attitude says it all."

"I'm here, aren't I?"

"Only because your ego is bruised. If I had attended that meeting today, even if I'd said the same things I've said tonight, would you have brought pizza and wine to my house? Or would you have celebrated your success somewhere more sophisticated and refined? With someone more up to *your* standards?"

When he didn't have an instant comeback, Ruth Ann knew she'd hit on the truth. She walked to the front door and opened it. "Good night, Jonah."

He stared at her for a moment, then gave a slight shrug. "Whatever you say." His long strides took him past her, then across the small stone stoop and down the steps. Ruth Ann closed the door and locked it.

She was still standing in the living room, rubbing her hands over her arms, trying to feel warm, trying to feel normal, when the doorbell rang. Hard to believe she'd have two visitors in one night—most people met her at the barn.

But it was Jonah who stood on the porch. "I forgot something."

"Oh." She backed up. "Come in."

"Thank you."

He stalked past her and she shut the door quickly, because the cold air coming through chilled the wooden floor. In just a few minutes, she would be free to find some socks, curl up in her bed under a couple of blankets, and be perfectly miserable.

When she turned around, though, Jonah stood right behind her, so close she had to look up to meet his gaze. "What did you forget?" Ruth Ann asked, just to have something to say.

"This."

He lifted a hand and brushed her hair behind her shoulder with the backs of his fingers. Without pause or hesitation, his palm cupped the nape of her neck, the flesh warm and firm against hers. His touch alone held her motionless.

Then he bent his head and kissed her. His mouth moved over hers with deliberate sensuality, his experience and skill coaxing the response she really didn't want to give.

But as soon as she surrendered, as soon as she kissed him back, desperation took control. Ruth Ann submitted to her own needs, her desire to give this one man everything. He backed her up against the wall and leaned into her, his arms hard around her waist, his lips seeking all the pleasure points on her neck and shoulders, his body rigid in her embrace. She thought—hoped—he would take her right where they stood.

But Jonah had no such intent. Before he could lose the last shred of control, he jerked his head back, breathing hard.

"As far as I'm concerned, there's something important between us," he muttered, pushing himself away from Ruth Ann. "Something unrelated to barns and schools and horses. Or even Darcy. I came here tonight because I wanted more."

"More…what?" she whispered, looking absolutely bewildered.

Jonah rubbed his hands over his face. "More of *you*. Your energy, your certainty, the focus and power you can call on, the strength you used with Waldo this afternoon."

"It's just riding. It's what I do."

"I know you think that's all you have to offer other people, a set of skills and years of experience." He backed up a few steps, putting a safe distance between them. "And until you realize how much you are, how much you can bring to a relationship…well, I guess I'm just plain out of luck."

Shaking his head, he stepped to the door and turned the knob. As he crossed the threshold, he glanced back over his shoulder. "The sooner you could figure it out, though, the more time we could enjoy being together. Life doesn't last forever, Ruth Ann. Don't waste too much of what we could have."

The door panel thudded into the frame as Jonah shut himself outside. This time, he didn't go back.

WITH JAYNE'S approval and Miriam's grudging assent, Ruth Ann told her students about the Hawkridge Horse Show. The girls reacted with enthusiasm bordering on hysteria and volunteered for every phase of preparation and execution. They also tried to expand their lesson schedules to fill more hours than Ruth Ann could fit into a day.

"I don't think I'll be ready to jump on Dusty by Thanksgiving," Darcy commented as they finished up her lesson on Thursday. "Do you think you might have another show next spring?"

Ruth Ann put an arm around the girl's shoulders and gave her a squeeze as they walked to the barn. "You're not getting off that easy. Not every class will require jumping. We'll have Walk/Trot and Go-As-You-Please classes, so you and Dusty will definitely be part of the action. Your only decision is whether you want to canter or not."

"Awesome!" Darcy gave it some thought. "I'll ride Saturday and Sunday this week, and then on Monday at my lesson, I'll start working on the canter. Won't Jonah be surprised?"

With Darcy looking at her, Ruth Ann managed an encouraging smile. "He'll be impressed, to say the least."

He hadn't appeared for Darcy's lesson that afternoon, which was fine with Ruth Ann because she had no idea what she would say to him, despite a sleepless night spent thinking about his parting words.

Did he mean he wanted a relationship between them? Hard as that was to believe, she couldn't find another way to interpret what he'd said. *Something important* didn't sound like a one-night stand, a weekend fling, or even a mutually satisfying affair.

Ruth Ann had never let herself imagine Jonah as a significant part of her life. She'd long ago learned not to long for things she knew she couldn't have, like being thin and beautiful. Sure, she'd fantasized about sex with him, dreamed about having him in her bed…and in the barn, on the grass by a calm lake, at a ski lodge and just about any other romantic setting that came to mind. She'd thought they might get that far, at least. After all, he did keep kissing her.

How could they have a relationship, though, when they were still on opposite sides of the Hawkridge stable issue? Jonah had moved to Ridgeville and hoped to establish his business here—the Hawkridge project had to be important to that agenda. Would Jonah give up his professional involvement with Hawkridge for her?

Just as important to Ruth Ann was the preservation of the old stable and her family's historic connection to that building. Could she forget her principles, forget her threat to resign rather than work in a new barn, just to be with Jonah? Could she ask him to give up his standards to make her happy? There didn't seem to be any middle ground between them. What kind of relationship could they build, when one person had to lose and one person won?

Whenever she reached the end of her reasoning, she came up with the same unanswerable question. But Jonah didn't call even once over the weekend, so she didn't have to provide him with an answer she didn't have.

Luckily, the paperwork involved in setting up a show kept her occupied in the minutes when she didn't have a student begging for a lesson to prepare for the show. Ruth Ann had invited riders from several other private schools and barns in the area, just to be sure they had an interesting mix of horses and riders. Setting up the class schedules alone was a complicated task. She was also making equipment lists, soliciting judges and officials for the day of the show, and trying to figure out what physical repairs had to be made to the stable so that the parents and guests would leave with a favorable impression of the Hawkridge equestrian program.

Her luck ran out on Monday afternoon. Indian summer had arrived, and the warm cloudless days turned the horses lazy and sleepy, so Dusty didn't feel like trotting, letting alone cantering for Darcy.

"That's the downside of a quiet pony," Ruth Ann told her. "He can be stubborn about being anything else."

"But I only have six more lessons before the show. How will we get enough practice?"

"The weather will change in a few days, and he'll be fresh again. For now, just get him into a smooth trot and practice your posting. Remember, rise with the outside front foot."

As she watched Darcy go around the arena, she caught sight of Jonah observing from a shaded place on the wall of the stable yard. He lifted a hand in greeting, and she gave him a nod before turning to keep her eyes on horse and rider.

Would he want to talk, once the girls left? What would she say?

Once Darcy dismounted, though, Jonah stood talking to her and to the other girls working around her, leaving Ruth Ann free to continue with her chores. He didn't offer to help. She wasn't sure she would be happier if he had, but after all her claims of independence, she could scarcely ask for assistance.

In fact she got so busy, feeding and moving horses, cleaning stalls, that she hardly noticed as the girls left for dinner and the barn quieted down. Coming back with Snowflake, the last of the horses to move that day, Ruth Ann actually thought she again had the place to herself, until one shadow in the hallway separated itself from the others.

"So you decided to go ahead with the show," he said.

She swallowed hard. "Jayne loved the idea, and the girls are having a good time getting ready."

Hands in the pockets of his slacks, Jonah followed her down the aisle to Snowflake's stall. "Miriam didn't."

When she glanced at him, she saw the glint of his grin in the dim light. "She complained to you?"

"We were meeting to talk about the stable project, and she brought up the subject."

Ruth Ann slipped off Snowflake's halter and backed out of the stall…right into Jonah.

Stumbling forward, she slammed her shoulder against the wall and lurched around. "Sorry."

He steadied her with his hands on her upper arms. "Are you okay?"

"Sure. Sure, I'm fine." Except she was having trouble catching her breath, being so close to him.

He loosened his hold, but didn't let go. Instead, his hands soothed her, sliding gently up and down. "I didn't mean to trip you."

"You didn't. I'm just clumsy." She sounded as if she'd just ridden the Kentucky Derby winner around the track twice.

"Only when you're nervous." She could hear the amusement in his voice. "Why are you always nervous around me, Ruth Ann?"

"Because I don't know what you want!"

Horrified to hear what she'd just said, she clapped her hands over her mouth.

Jonah let his hands fall to his sides and gazed at her for a minute. He took a deep breath. "I want only what you want to give," he said in a low voice.

Since she didn't know what to say, wasn't sure what that was, they stood in silence for another long moment.

"Well." Jonah stirred and put his hands back in his pockets. "I thought I'd ask what I could do to help with the horse show, since it was essentially my suggestion. I should have some free time over the next several weeks, so I'd be happy to do whatever I can."

Trying to bring her brain back to a functional state, Ruth Ann headed toward the lounge, hanging up Snowflake's halter on the way.

"Has Eve been back to visit Snowflake?" Jonah asked from behind her.

"I see her here some afternoons, when it's really busy and she thinks no one's noticed." Ruth Ann flipped on all the overhead lights as she passed through the doorway. "But she doesn't talk to anyone else." At the huge cork board where she'd tacked up the various papers relating to the upcoming show, she located the list of building chores she thought should be addressed.

"I'd like the place to look presentable, of course," she told Jonah. "These are things I thought would make a difference." She handed him the sheet. "There might be other ideas I missed. If you'd like to take on that project—"

He nodded, looking over her suggestions. "Good ideas all of them. Do you have permission to use Hector and Ruben again? We might need a crew."

"I imagine Jayne would let us borrow them. She's expecting all the students and teachers to attend, though it's not required, of course."

"I bet they will. Where are they all going to sit?"

When she stared at him blankly, he pulled a pen out of his pocket. "Right. I'll put that on the list."

With his note made, he looked at her again. "I'll get this stuff underway and be in touch."

"Thanks."

He walked to the outside door, but turned around before he touched the knob. "Ruth Ann, about what I said last week…"

She couldn't force a sound past the lump in her throat.

"I'm not taking anything back—I meant every word. But I'm not so dense I don't see the barriers. Some of them, anyway. I think we could get past them, but I understand how tough the choices are."

As if he'd touched her, she felt the desire and need between them. She wanted to cross the room, let Jonah fold his arms around her and dissolve her fears, her doubts.

His cell phone rang. He swore, pulled it out of his pocket and heard his former business partner's voice blaring. "Stephen, I can't talk now. I'll call you back."

When he looked at Ruth Ann again, Jonah could tell he'd lost the battle.

She gave him a sad smile. "We both need some time to think about what you said. Maybe after the show, over the holiday…" She let her voice trail off, and he understood what she was trying not to say.

Nothing would have changed, and they both knew it.

"Right." He felt for the doorknob behind him, turned it and stepped out backwards. "I'll call in a day or two when I've got some progress to report."

"Thank you, Jonah."

"Sure." He waved and shut the door, walked to his truck without thinking beyond the next step or two. He managed to keep his mind blank all the way home.

Then he walked into the kitchen, filled a glass with ice, took down the Scotch bottle and went to sit in the dark parlor while he contemplated the conundrum his life had become.

If he stuck with the new stable, he'd lose Ruth Ann. If he ditched the new stable, he'd lose his business. Maybe he was spoiled, but Jonah really didn't believe he couldn't find a way to have both.

When he stumbled to bed, half a bottle and several hours later, he'd developed an inkling of an answer. Not a guarantee, he knew. At this point, however, it was his only shot at happiness.

He'd completely forgotten to return Stephen's call.

HALLOWEEN came and went, with the appropriate festivities at Hawkridge—the dining hall decorated with cobwebs, spiders and bats, scary skits and dancing, teachers in their classrooms offering goodies for trick-or-treaters.

Meanwhile, Hector and Ruben spent hours washing down walls at the barn, adding colorful chrysanthemums to the landscaping, building and painting jumps. Jonah brought a termite inspector and a construction engineer out on a day when Jayne guaranteed Ruth Ann would attend a faculty meeting. The news was as bad as he'd feared, though the barn wasn't in imminent danger of collapse, but he decided not to burden Ruth Ann with the results until after the show. She was looking exhausted already, with shadows under her eyes and hollows in her cheeks. He would swear she'd lost weight. And so he kept trying to help, hoping to make her feel better and ease the load she carried.

He worked with Hector and Ruben to brace the worst of the damaged walls, using paint to camouflage the repairs. They worked on the tricky stall locks and sticky sliding doors, scrubbed the aisle floors and brick walls.

In the evenings, Jonah went home to his drafting table and the book he'd borrowed from the Hawkridge library. His inkling had turned into a plan. His plan, he hoped, would convince Ruth Ann they could have everything…together.

As he worked around the barn, he got the chance to observe Darcy at her lessons and with the other girls. She'd changed radically from the quiet mouse he'd left at the school in September. She laughed and smiled, teased and argued, and rode Dusty as if she'd been born in the saddle. Her cantering continued to improve, especially once the weather broke and Dusty decided he could move at something faster than a walk.

Darcy's physique had changed, too. She stood up straight, no longer trying to hide her body and avoid anyone's notice. Jonah wasn't sure how much weight she'd lost, but her jeans and breeches rode lightly over her muscles now. Her arms showed shape, and she was up to cleaning four stalls every day.

Then the real bad news hit with just a week to go before the show, when he answered his cell phone on Friday night without looking at the number first.

"Hi, Jonah. How are you?"

He blew a frustrated breath. "Busy, Brittany. What can I do for you?"

"I just wanted to let you know when I'd be arriving."

"Arriving?" Dread coiled in his gut.

"Why, of course. I received an invitation to this cute little horse show they're throwing at Darcy's school, and I couldn't resist coming to watch."

Jonah suddenly realized he had a very big headache. He propped an elbow on his desk and pressed his forehead against his palm. "Terrific. I think you'll be pleased with how Darcy's doing. She looks good. I think she's happy."

"Lovely. I understand you've bought yourself a house in— what is it? Hickville? And you're operating your business there, now."

"Ridgeville. That's right."

"How quaint."

"You must have been talking to Stephen." Years ago, Brittany had introduced him to Stephen and suggested they form a partnership.

"We keep in touch. You'll have room for me to stay at your place, I assume."

"That would be a very bad assumption. I do not have room

for you. There's a nice hotel in town. I'll make your reservation, if you'd like."

"But—" She stopped, probably deciding that pushing him would be a bad idea. "That would be kind of you, Jonah. I'll come in on Wednesday and stay until Monday morning. It's been an intense trip, so I'll be glad for a few days to relax. I hope you'll let me take you to dinner while I'm there." She paused for just the right length of time. "There are restaurants in this paradise, aren't there? I mean, where one can get a civilized meal?"

"Yes, Brittany. There's a very good pizza parlor." Jonah grinned as she gasped. "Gotta go." He disconnected before he could hear her protest, and didn't answer when she called back immediately.

He ought to warn Darcy, just in case Brittany decided to be cute and make her visit a "surprise." Ruth Ann, too, would need to know. There could be no predicting what Brittany might take it into her head to do or say.

In fact, he decided, Ruth Ann needed to know tonight. For weeks now, he'd worked his butt off around the barn, while trying hard to keep things between the two of them cool and uncomplicated. The effort had cost him many a night's sleep.

He'd take her some dinner, make her laugh, see if they could find an insignificant rule to break together. No pressure, no demands. Just a nice evening between friends.

With the prospect of yet another cold shower for Jonah at the end of it.

Chapter Twelve

Ruth Ann woke up to a wonderful aroma—bacon, she thought, and cheese and bread. Breakfast? Who would be making breakfast?

She forced her eyes open and realized she'd fallen asleep on the sofa in the barn lounge, still wearing her boots, her warm jacket, even her hat. And she still smelled bacon.

When she moved, a voice across the room said, "Wake up, Sleeping Beauty. We've got a royal feast here, and I'm starving."

"Jonah?" She sat up, blinking, and let her feet drop to the floor. "What time is it?"

"Eight-thirty." When she continued to stare at him in confusion, he clarified. "Friday night."

"Oh." So she hadn't slept through until morning. "What are you doing here?"

"Bringing you dinner. Which is ready, by the way." He came to the sofa and held out his hands. "Up."

Still groggy, she put her palms over his and let him pull her to her feet. His hands were so warm, and he felt so strong, steadying her as she got her balance. All she wanted to do was lean into him.

But dinner did smell awfully good. "Did you cook? Here?"

Jonah laughed and shook his head. "Oh, no. The café special tonight was spaghetti carbonara, so I picked up some carry-out and a bottle of wine. Come and eat."

He led her to the table with one hand and pulled out her chair with the other, then slipped her coat off her shoulders and removed her hat. The delicious fragrance that had wakened her rose from a huge bowl filled with pasta tossed with bits of bacon and cheese. As Jonah took over, serving their plates, pouring the wine, Ruth Ann didn't argue. She, too, wanted to eat.

They caught up on their planning for the show over dinner, although there were long silences while they simply enjoyed the delicious food. Jonah had brought a salad and dessert, too—a deep, rich chocolate mousse. Sitting back after the last bite, Ruth Ann sighed in contentment.

"That's definitely the most elegant food this room has ever seen. What a wonderful dinner, Jonah. Thanks."

"My pleasure. I'm glad you enjoyed it." He took a sip of wine, set his glass down and then continued to turn the stem with his fingers. "I thought I'd better let you know ahead of time—Darcy's mother will be coming to the horse show."

"Oh." She wasn't sure what he wanted her to understand. "That's good…isn't it?"

He shook his head. "I doubt it. I mean, it sounds like a good idea, mother coming to see daughter ride in the show. But more often than not, Brittany manages to turn events like this into a soul-destroying scene."

"That's the last thing Darcy needs. She's doing so well."

"Right. Maybe this will be one of Brittany's rare good days. But I wanted to warn you, so you could avoid her if at all possible."

"Great. One more challenge on an already impossible day."

Ruth Ann got up to clear the disposable plastic plates off the table. "I appreciate the heads-up, though. I'll stay out of her way, if I can."

"So will I, though I suspect she'll hunt me down." He packed the left-over pasta and salad into boxes. "She expected to stay at my house while she was here." His tone indicated what he thought of the idea.

"Presumptuous lady."

"That's Brittany." He put the boxes in the refrigerator and shut the door. "So, are you planning to sleep here for the rest of the night, or can I walk you home?"

Ruth Ann wanted to be strong. She knew she should decline the offer, send Jonah on his way and go back to work on her show lists for a couple of hours before heading home. Or, as happened more often these last weeks, falling asleep again on the couch. Some nights, she didn't have the heart to go back to her empty house and get into her emptier bed.

But he looked so good, in his jeans and a bulky sweater, his hair falling light and loose across his forehead. He smiled at her, his bright blue gaze encouraging, warm, and held out his hand.

Just this once. Ruth Ann grinned. "Sure."

She donned her coat again, but left the hat on the counter, turned off the lamps he'd switched on and joined him at the door, slipping her hand into his waiting one.

Without releasing her fingers, Jonah stepped through the doorway and waited while she locked up. They strolled across the parking area and into the trees, following the path worn by her students as they walked back and forth between the barn and the school. Words didn't seem necessary in the cold autumn darkness. Ruth Ann felt completely satisfied just to be walking beside Jonah, to have spent some time with him that wasn't about business but about simply enjoying each other.

The rear of her little blue cottage faced the barn, so she led the way through the back gate and across the garden, dormant now in preparation for winter. After feeling one-handed for the key she kept under a flower pot, she unlocked the kitchen door. Then, with a deep breath, she turned to Jonah.

"I appreciate the escort. It was a lovely walk."

"Peaceful," he agreed. Somehow, he now held both her hands in both of his. "I've enjoyed the whole evening."

"Me, too." They were spinning this out, she thought, trying to avoid saying goodbye. She didn't want him to go, but at some point, surely, he'd leave. "You should—"

"I should," Jonah said. He leaned forward, then, and kissed her, walking her backwards and kicking the kitchen door shut behind him.

Long minutes of soft, aching kisses followed that first one, as mouth clung to mouth, needing each touch more than they needed air to breathe. Ruth Ann's knees went weak, and she fell back a step, searching for support against a nearby wall or counter. Jonah followed, releasing her hands to put his arms around her waist. The balance shifted, and he became her support, leaning back himself and pulling her body up against his.

Flat against round, hard against soft—the differences between them ignited a brighter, deeper desire. Ruth Ann pressed closer, moved against him, and Jonah groaned in response. His hands curved over her hips, cupped her bottom, while she slipped her hands under his sweater to slide her palms across the bare skin of his waist.

"Ruth Ann." Jonah lifted his head, trying for control, which became impossible when she dragged her mouth across his throat and teased his skin with her tongue. "Ahh, woman." He endured—enjoyed—her caress for as long as he could bear. "I can't—" He drew a shuddering breath. "I have to stop, or I won't be able to."

She bit gently on his earlobe. "Don't. Stop."

A gentleman would ask her if she were sure. A thoughtful man would give her a chance to calm down, let her make the decision with a clear head. A good man would not take advantage of a woman under the influence of desire.

Jonah realized in that moment he was neither good, nor thoughtful, nor a gentleman. He hadn't come here tonight to seduce Ruth Ann. But he couldn't refuse the opportunity, now that she'd offered.

And so he lowered his chin and took her mouth with his, unleashing the need he'd been trying to control. He pushed her coat off her shoulders, stroked the backs of his fingers down either side of her spine, then lifted the hem of her sweatshirt to find another layer of cloth tucked into the waist of her breeches.

"You wear too damn many clothes," he growled against her lips.

She gave a surprised laugh. "It's cold in the barn."

"It's hot in here." His fingertips reached skin, finally, and he forgot to breathe as he explored her soft flesh, stroking circles from her waist in ever widening paths, exploring the dip of her spine, her shoulder blades and ribs. "So smooth. So sweet." He took hold of the cloth covering her and pulled it off.

"Jonah!" She crossed her arms over her breasts. "I'm not—I mean—"

"You're gorgeous." He saw her shiver and wrapped his arms around her. "But maybe cold?" Ruth Ann nodded, and he nodded back at her. "Let's go somewhere I can warm you up."

With a deep breath she turned and led him toward the back

of the house, to a dark room in which Jonah sensed rather than saw the bed. Ruth Ann didn't turn on the light, and though he wanted to, he resisted the urge. He would love her first, convince her how beautiful he thought she was, and then persuade her to let him see as well as touch.

She wasn't quite as shy as he expected, though, because when she turned to face him, she'd unfastened the front clasp on her bra, letting the straps slip off her shoulders and down her arms to vanish at their feet.

"Ah. Nice," he managed. Placing his hands over her collarbones, he warmed her skin with his palms, stroking along her breast bone with his thumbs, letting them meet over the pulse beating fast at the hollow of her throat. Ruth Ann circled her arms over his shoulders and took a step forward, offering her mouth for a kiss. And then, as their mouths got busy and their bodies warmed, Jonah let his hands slide down, slowly, gently, until he could cup her breasts in his hands.

Sensation consumed him. Need devoured him and he shook with the effort to keep control, to coax her slowly to the point of no return. Ruth Ann wasn't helping his cause, not when she jerked his sweater up and off, over his head, not when she swayed her hips into him time and time again, and not when she clasped him around the waist and locked the skin of his belly and ribs against hers.

Jonah retained enough sense to realize he had to get her boots off before he lay beside her on the bed.

"Sit," he ordered, gritting his teeth and swearing as he tugged on one leather obstruction and then the other. He removed his own socks and shoes while he was at it. And when he turned to Ruth Ann, he found she'd removed her breeches for him. She lay across the bed, waiting, wearing a pair of plain white panties that seemed to Jonah the ultimate erotic invitation.

He came to her then, stretched out beside her and gave himself over to all the fantasies he'd indulged over the weeks he'd known her. She had him out of his jeans soon enough. In a matter of moments, his boxers went onto the floor, along with those panties, and it was just the two of them, skin to skin, hands free to roam, skin heating, sweating, with whispers and moans as background music.

He went back to his jeans for his wallet and the condoms he'd been carrying for almost as long as he'd known Ruth Ann. When he bent over her, she looked a little scared, more nervous than excited.

"Have you been with somebody before?" Jonah asked. He'd never considered the possibility she was a virgin.

To his relief, she nodded. "It's been a long time. And it— it wasn't…very good."

Jonah grinned and gave her a wink. "That's because you weren't with me." Then he set out to prove it.

Ruth Ann lost track of time, and space, even her own name as Jonah used his hands and his mouth, his tongue and his breath and his body to explain just why being loved by him was different than with anyone else. He eased himself inside her, and the sensation of their bodies joining generated a huge wave of warmth that pulsed up and out, through every inch of her. As he moved the waves began to build, to roar, to crash and she cried out, over and over again, at the ecstasy Jonah brought her. Seconds later, his body stiffened in her arms and he made a sound of his own, part pain, part pleasure. She held him tight, felt him shake.

Then he relaxed with a sigh, falling to the side while gathering her tightly against him.

"Fantastic," he murmured, kissing her forehead. "You're amazing."

Ruth Ann chuckled. "You said it was different—perfect—because of you."

He yawned. "You might not have noticed, but I'm an arrogant SOB." With the next breath, he fell asleep.

What surprised Ruth Ann most was that she did, too.

RUTH ANN opened her eyes as usual at five on Saturday morning. Quite wonderfully different, though, was the warm male body curved spoon-like around hers. She smiled, savoring last night's memories and this moment's sweet sensations. Given the choice, she wouldn't move another muscle for several hours. And she wouldn't wake Jonah until he woke himself up.

But work awaited her. The horses needed to be fed at six so they would be ready to start lessons at eight. With a sigh, she turned in his arms to face him, and put a hand on the blanket over his hip. "Jonah." She whispered, as if someone might hear. "Jonah, it's morning. Time to wake up."

"Mmm." He smiled without opening his eyes and tightened the arm around her shoulders, pulling her closer. "And what a great morning it is." His voice was husky, totally sexy. Near her arm, his body came to life, letting her know exactly what he was thinking.

"Yes, but—" She kissed his chin, lingered to taste the strong line of his jaw, then homed in on his lips. His hands moved under the blankets, finding and reawakening all her most sensitive places.

Ruth Ann decided the horses could eat at six-thirty.

An hour later, she didn't have to explain to Jonah the reasons she thought he ought to leave early. "I think we did a hell of a job of rule-breaking last night," he told her, holding her for a few final kisses before he went out the back door.

"Which rule is that?"

"I'm sure there's one on the books about teachers entertaining the opposite sex in their campus housing."

Ruth Ann felt the blush start on her chest to rise rapidly up her throat and across her cheeks. "There is, actually. In the contract." She covered her face with her hands. "I can't believe it. I broke an authentic, honest-to-goodness rule!" She looked up at Jonah, laughing. "Isn't that wonderful?"

"You're wonderful." He kissed her again. "And I'm out of here. See you later." One last touch of his mouth to hers, and he stepped out the door.

The hungry horses were kicking walls and banging buckets when she reached the barn half an hour later. "Well, I'm sorry," she said as she poured grain into Waldo's dish. "But I think one night of personal life in thirty-odd years should be allowed."

She leaned against his side as he nose-dived into his food. "Oh, Waldo, he was so wonderful. Everything I'd ever imagined it might be. So strong and gentle, and he takes such care—"

She daydreamed for a few minutes, until Snowflake whinnied, requesting her breakfast. "Yes, ma'am," Ruth Ann called, hurrying back to the feed room. "At your beck and call, ma'am. As always."

Once the day got started, the work didn't stop. She was cleaning stalls when students began to arrive for lessons, and lessons had been scheduled every hour all day long. With the show exactly a week away, all the girls were in a state of high anxiety. Ruth Ann gave each of them the same little speech.

"This show is just for fun. Yes, there will be ribbons. But win or lose, what I want is for everyone to enjoy the day and the chance to spend time in a beautiful place with their favorite horse."

Most of the girls nodded and went away calmer. Darcy,

however, came to her lesson with a set face and rode like a wooden puppet, to the point where even Dusty was beginning to look over his shoulder, confused by her behavior.

Ruth Ann finally stopped her at the farthest point of the arena from the barn and walked over to stand looking up into the girl's face. "What's wrong, Darcy? What are you thinking about today?"

Hands clenched tightly on the reins, Darcy didn't say anything for a minute. "My mother's coming. To the show."

"Your stepdad mentioned that to me."

"I can't do this," Darcy said. "I can't ride with her watching."

"Why not?"

"I—I'll mess up. I'll fall off. I know it. Can you take my name off the entry list? I'll come and watch with her, but I can't ride."

Ruth Ann crossed her arms over her chest, noticing that her breasts felt tender. She blocked the reason out of her mind. "You think somehow it will be better if your mother knows that you were afraid to ride in the show because she was here?"

Darcy nodded emphatically. "Yes."

"Instead of, say, simply riding as you'd planned to, having a good time, and letting whatever she might say go in one ear and out the other?"

Now the girl gazed at her in doubt. "You're saying she's going to be a problem whether I ride or don't ride?"

"I think it's possible. What do you suppose she will say if you drop out?"

Darcy pondered the question for a minute, staring at Dusty's twitching ears. Then she looked at Ruth Ann. "That could be really awful. At least if I ride, I won't have to be with her during the classes I would have shown in."

"Exactly."

"And since I'm supposed to help the judge during some of the other classes, I won't have to sit with her then, either."

"That's a plus."

Darcy took a deep breath. "Okay. I'll ride. Let me see if I can do better for the rest of today."

"I couldn't ask for more."

The rest of the day passed in the same flurry of lessons and work. Ruth Ann was constantly aware of Jonah on the edge of her vision, working with Hector and Ruben to put the finishing touches on a set of bleachers he'd acquired somewhere, the arena fencing, the jumps and dressage markers. She took the time to ride Waldo, and caught Jonah watching her while she practiced.

They didn't get a chance to talk about anything but the show until after dark, after the horses were fed and moved, after the barn was locked for the night. They walked through the woods again, taking the leftover pasta with them and sharing it for dinner in her kitchen, before spending the long, dark and lovely night together in her bed.

Sunday was another busy day, and Jonah left for home once dark arrived, saying he wanted her to get a decent night's sleep before the week started. Something about the way he said it, the implication that he wouldn't let her sleep if he stayed again, made her bed seem less empty.

The fact that he called when he got home and they talked for two hours while they each ate a peanut butter and jelly sandwich for dinner didn't hurt.

Ruth Ann spent Monday and Tuesday preparing all the papers necessary to produce a horse show—judges' evaluation sheets, class lists, score sheets, prize lists and programs for spectators. Jayne Thomas visited her at the copy machine and asked how things were going.

"Good," Ruth Ann said, watching the pages slide out of the slot. "Really good."

Jayne tilted her head and looked at her. "You seem…different."

"Nope. Same old me." But even to herself, Ruth Ann sounded breathless. And different.

"You're pretty relaxed, for someone about to pull off a really big event like this."

"It's a show. I've been to enough of them, I ought to be able to organize one in my sleep." Was she blushing at the mention of sleep?

"Okay, okay. I'll take your word for it." But Jayne wore a speculative look as she left the room.

Jonah called Monday and Tuesday nights. On Tuesday, he reminded Ruth Ann about Brittany. "Remember, she'll be in the area sometime tomorrow. I hope she leaves you alone, but you never know. If she shows up, don't kill her if you can help it."

"I'll be a perfect lady," she assured him.

"Hah," Jonah said.

RUTH ANN worked through a pouring rain all day on Wednesday. The weather kept the girls away and she used the time she would have been teaching for more last-minute work on the show and the barn. Jonah, Hector and Ruben had repaired the roof, so she didn't need as many buckets as she once had to catch the leaks.

But the horses who spent the night outside came in wet and filthy. The grays who went out during the day soon looked the same. In the process of rubbing the animals down, a good percentage of the dirt transferred from their coats to Ruth Ann's clothes and body.

She'd just finished feeding the grays in the late afternoon

when she heard a car engine cut off outside the barn. Hoping for Jonah, she hurried to the lounge and used a wet paper towel to wipe off her face and hands. For the first time ever in her life, she wished she had a mirror somewhere in the barn to check her hair.

She didn't have time to change her breeches, but she did pull off the dirt-smeared sweatshirt, leaving her a little chilly in just a black turtleneck shirt. With luck, Jonah would take care of that problem.

But when she went to the front of the barn, the figure silhouetted against the rain bore no resemblance to her tall, lean lover.

Ruth Ann stopped in her tracks. "Can I help you?"

The woman stepped into the light. She wore a raincoat that hung in elegant folds from her shoulders to the high heels of her boots. Her shiny brown hair clung like a cap to her small head, with light wisps escaping to feather around her high cheekbones and graceful neck.

Her dark gaze surveyed Ruth Ann from head to toes and back again, and her perfectly made-up lips twisted to the side. "I'm looking for the stable manager." The New Jersey accent identified her as easily as if she wore a nametag.

"That would be me. Ruth Ann Blakely." She extended her arm, offering a handshake.

Brittany Granger pushed her hands a little deeper into the pockets of the raincoat. "Really." She looked Ruth Ann over again. "I'm Darcy's mother."

Ruth Ann let her hand fall to her side. "I thought you might be. Darcy looks like you."

"Not really." Now she turned her head from side to side, assessing the barn. "Is this the school's primary stable?"

"Yes." Ruth Ann stiffened her spine and took hold of her

temper. "Howard Ridgely built this stable when he built the main house, and it's served the estate's horses ever since."

"Pity." Brittany sniffed through her tiny nose. "I would think the situation would have been rectified before now."

"It's not a situation. It's a perfectly functional stable." She remembered she'd told Jonah she would not kill Darcy's mother. "Would you like to look at the horses?"

In the silence that followed, the distinct drip of water into the buckets under the roof leaks could be heard.

Brittany shook her head. "I don't think that's necessary. I've seen all I care to." With a swirl of that coat, she pivoted on one pointed toe and walked out into the rain.

"So have I," Ruth Ann muttered. "So have I."

Chapter Thirteen

Jonah worked until 4:00 a.m. on Thursday morning before falling into an exhausted coma on the couch in his office. The scent of brewing coffee penetrated his consciousness slowly but surely. He smiled, thinking that sharing a cup of coffee with Ruth Ann would be a terrific way to start the morning.

Then he woke up all the way and realized there was no way Ruth Ann would be at his house early in the morning. He knew he hadn't set up the brewing machine the night before. So where was the aroma coming from?

As he descended the stairs in his socks, a glance at the fur-trimmed leather jacket hanging on the hat rack in the front hall gave him the warning he needed. By the time he reached the kitchen at the back of the house, he'd prepared himself for the worst.

And there she was, standing at the counter pouring coffee into two of his mugs as if she owned the place. A snug black sweater and black leather pants revealed her slender, athletic figure. He thought her chest seemed more ample than he remembered, her face smoother. Had she been jumping horses in Europe, or having cosmetic surgery?

Jonah didn't care one way or the other. "Brittany, what the

hell are you doing here at—" he squinted at the clock "—seven-thirty in the morning?" Three hours of sleep. No wonder his head felt stuffed with sawdust.

"I thought we could have breakfast together," she said, as if they were the best of friends. Or maybe something more. "I brought doughnuts, which is the closest thing to pastries around here, and picked up some fresh-ground coffee. I knew you'd have a coffeemaker." She held out one of the mugs she'd poured. "You couldn't survive without your brew."

He took the cup but didn't drink. "I don't want to have breakfast with you. I don't want you in my house."

"Oh, Jonah, calm down. It's just a friendly morning meeting. Let's sit down and catch up." She seated herself at the kitchen table and chose a powdered sugar doughnut off the plate sitting there.

Jonah hesitated, then went to join her. There was no point in kicking her out—she wouldn't leave until she was good and ready. "What do we have to catch up on?"

Brittany blotted white powder off her lips. "My flight from Europe was fine, thank you. Rather long, adding the extra leg from New York to North Carolina. The room you reserved for me is adequate. I'm surprised the accommodations in this part of the world are so good. I slept well last night."

"I'm so glad to hear that."

She ignored his sarcasm. "As soon as I got into town, of course, I drove out to Darcy's school. You won't believe this, but the headmistress wouldn't allow me to take Darcy out of class so we could visit. She gave me a tour of the empty classrooms and basically threw me out into the rain. Honestly!"

Jonah didn't waste time on false sympathy. He was afraid he knew what was coming next. "Then where did you go?"

"To the stable, of course. Darcy has written about very little other than her riding coach, and I wanted to meet this paragon."

"And did you?" At least Ruth Ann hadn't hit her on the head with a horseshoe and hidden the body.

"I met *someone*." Brittany shrugged her shoulders. "Someone claiming to be the stable manager—an odd woman who didn't appear to know enough to wear a decent coat in the rain. Is this person responsible, Jonah? I mean, is she really an appropriate person to ensure the girls' safety?"

"Ruth Ann is a perfectly normal adult. She'd probably been working. You wouldn't know this, but hard work warms you up."

Brittany slowly lowered the remains of her doughnut to a napkin on the table. "You're quite passionate in your defense of this Ruth Ann person."

"She's a great teacher. Darcy's made a lot of progress while working with Ruth Ann and her horses. You should be grateful, not making snide comments."

"I see." Her brown eyes had narrowed to slits between lashes heavy with black mascara. "You and Ruth Ann are friends."

"I've been working on the stable this last month, getting ready for the show." He shrugged, pretending indifference. "I've seen her with the students and I know what a good job she does. That's all."

"I thought you were designing a new stable for the school. Wasn't that the point of being here?"

"I *am* designing a new stable. But it wouldn't be ready for this show, obviously."

"This Ruth Ann, she's helping you with the plans? It's important to consult with the person who'll be working in the stable, you know. We each have our own way of caring for the horses."

"Yes, I know." He got to his feet. "I've got to get to work, Brittany. If you—"

She didn't move. "You work from your house now, Jonah. No more tantrums from Stephen if you aren't in the office by eight. Sit down and relax."

"No." He'd taken as much as he could handle. Rounding the table, Jonah closed his hand around her upper arm and lifted her out of the chair. "Time to go, Brittany."

She didn't fight him. In fact, she came up easily and moved into him. "It's good to see you again, Jonah. You're looking younger, more energetic than the last time we met." Her hand stroked circles over the center of his chest.

"Mountain air." Keeping hold of her arm, he walked her to the front hall. "I'll see you at the show on Saturday, I'm sure."

"How about dinner tonight?"

"Busy."

"Jonah, you have to eat." She slid her arms into the fur-trimmed jacket he held out. "Make reservations and pick me up at the hotel at seven."

He opened the door. "I have other plans."

"No, you don't." Walking by, she trailed her hand across his cheek. "See you later."

"No, you won't." Jonah closed the door behind her and leaned back against it, rubbing his hands over his face.

Had she always been this way? Was this the behavior he'd thought was "super-sexy?" What kind of deluded fool had he been? Needing a strong shot of reality, he grabbed the nearest phone and dialed the Hawkridge stable number. He could only hope Ruth Ann would hear—

"You've reached The Hawkridge School Stables. Please leave a message."

He groaned. "I wanted to rescind the request not to murder Darcy's mother. Give me a call when you get a chance."

Hanging up, he wondered what the weekend would bring. If Brittany didn't get her way, she was perfectly capable of creating a public firestorm that would embarrass everyone within earshot.

Maybe he should take her to dinner, just to keep her in a good mood. He wouldn't enjoy a second of the process, but he might be able to deflect her attention from Ruth Ann and Darcy.

Jonah didn't like the idea, but his attention might be the only defense between his ex-wife and the women he loved.

DARCY HURRIED to her room after the last class on Thursday, anxious to get into her riding clothes and rush over to the stable. Today was the last lesson before the show, her last chance to work on her canter with Dusty. Friday had been reserved for cleaning up horses, then saddles, bridles and boots. They wanted everything perfect for Saturday.

Eve was lying on her bed when Darcy opened the door. After dropping her books on her own mattress, Darcy looked at her roommate. "Are you okay?"

"Sure." But then she sighed.

Darcy pulled her breeches and a sweatshirt out of a drawer. "You don't sound okay."

"Got a note from my mom."

"What'd she say?"

"She's going to Aspen for Thanksgiving."

"You get to ski for Thanksgiving? Cool."

Eve shook her head. "I'm not going. Just her and the new boyfriend."

"Oh." Darcy knew the feeling. "Well, you wouldn't want to hang around with them anyway." She thought a minute. "You can come home with me. My dad would be glad to have you. He says he's got lots of room in this new house he bought."

Eve rolled over. "I'll probably just stay in bed. Why gorge yourself just to throw it all up again?"

"Good question." Darcy pulled her hair back into a ponytail. "Maybe you could not gorge, just eat normally."

"Or not eat at all."

"You're too skinny now." Pulling on her boots, Darcy tried once again. "Want to walk over to the barn with me? I've got a lesson. You could talk to Snowflake. You know Ms. Blakely doesn't mind."

Eve didn't answer, and Darcy shrugged. All she could do was ask.

When she stood up, though, Eve rolled over to sit up. "Wait a minute." She pulled on jeans over the tights she'd worn to class, jerked off her skirt and dragged a sweatshirt over her head, added socks and sneakers. "Okay, I'm ready."

After yesterday's rain, the ground was wet and the bare tree limbs dripped onto their heads as they walked through the woods. At the same time, the sky was a brilliant blue and sunlight poured like melted butter over rocks and buildings and fences. For once, the tops of the mountains were sharp and clear, without the usual mist to hide them.

And it was really cold. "Brrrr," Darcy said, opening the door to the stable lounge. "I should have brought my heavy gloves." Then she glanced toward the counter end of the room and the woman standing there. "Mom!" She swallowed hard. "You're here!"

"Hello, darling." Brittany was standing by the telephone and answering machine, holding out her arms. "I hoped you'd be at the barn this afternoon so I could say hello."

Darcy crossed the floor and gave her mother a hug. "What

a surprise." Remembering her etiquette lessons, she stepped back and turned halfway toward Eve. "Mom, this is my roommate, Eve Forrest. Eve, this is my mom, Brittany Granger."

"Well, hello." Darcy's mom walked toward Eve. "Aren't you beautiful?" With an arm around Eve's shoulders, Darcy's mom gave her a squeeze. "I'm glad to meet you."

"Hi," Eve said, with her usual shrug.

"Do you take lessons with Darcy?"

"No."

"She came along for a walk, Mom." Darcy took her helmet and riding gloves out of the cubby hole she used. "I've got to get tacked up."

"You go ahead. I'll be out in time for your lesson."

That, Darcy thought, *is what I'm afraid of.*

She had just settled herself into Dusty's saddle when she noticed Ms. Blakely frown in the direction of the barn. Darcy didn't have to look to see the problem.

"Start your warm-up," Ms. Blakely told her, turning her back to the approach of Darcy's mom. "Walk a couple of circles and then go into a slow trot. It's cold, so we want him thoroughly loosened up."

Darcy did as instructed. As she went around the arena, she couldn't help listening for the sound of voices as Ms. Blakely talked to her mom. Were they getting along? What was her mom saying?

She found out soon enough. "You're sitting too far back, Darcy," her mother called.

"She's fine," Ms. Blakely said. "Sit deep, Darcy. That's good."

A few minutes later, she heard, "Loosen the reins, darling. You're choking the horse."

"Keep contact with his mouth, Darcy. Light but firm."

As she rode by the two women, her mother turned to

Ms. Blakely. "Her stirrups are too long. She needs more bend in her knees."

"Her stirrups are just where we want them." Ms. Blakely's voice sounded like a wire stretched to its breaking point. "Okay, Darcy, when you're ready, pick up a canter."

Darcy took a deep breath, trying to remember everything she'd been practicing. Sit deep. Keep your heels down. Relax. Breathe. Don't pull back. "Dusty," she said, "canter!"

But Dusty ignored her. She tried again, with a tap of the whip. He bucked, tipping her forward in the saddle, and she gasped, looking toward her teacher.

"You're okay," Ms. Blakely said. "Just—"

At the same time, her mother cried out, "For God's sake, Darcy, use your whip to thrash that mule and canter!"

Darcy glanced at the other side of the arena and pulled Dusty to a halt.

Ms. Blakely had turned to her mother. Hands on her hips, she said, "I understand you would like to watch Darcy's lesson. But your comments are not helping her riding. Please sit down on one of the benches and stay quiet until the lesson is finished."

Her mother laughed. "Darcy does not need to learn to ride like a plowboy. If you can't teach her to sit properly, then I will."

"The result of your attempt to teach Darcy to ride was, I believe, a broken arm and a little girl afraid to try. At least I've been able to get her on the horse and moving through all the gaits."

"Hah. She can't even get that slug of a horse to canter."

Darcy cringed. It was bad enough that her mother was interfering with the lesson. But to use Darcy's lack of talent as a weapon against Dusty was just wrong. She could, too, canter. And she'd prove it.

First, she urged him into a strong trot, then kicked him and asked for a canter. He bucked again, but stayed in the trot. Darcy took a tight grip on the reins and the crop. "Canter!" she growled at the horse, kicking hard with her heels, giving him a hard slap with the whip.

Dusty got the message. He lifted his front end up and leaped into a fast canter, almost a gallop. Darcy dropped the whip, scrabbled for security, and ended up clutching two handfuls of mane to keep herself on. Moving with the horse's motion got harder and harder the faster he went, and the saddle started to feel like glass under her bottom. She couldn't remember what to do with her legs.

She wasn't sure what made Dusty slow down again but he did, enough that she could relax, sit back, and let go of his mane while they went down one side of the arena at a nice, slow canter. After a couple of minutes, she gently pulled the reins and he slowed even further into a trot and then a walk. Dusty and Darcy were both breathing hard as they walked around the arena and stopped next to Ms. Blakely and her mother.

"Well done," Ms. Blakely said. "I thought he was getting away from you, but you stuck on and brought him under control. That's terrific riding."

"You looked like a gypsy," Darcy's mother said. "Not a serious rider."

Ms. Blakely made a "time-out" sign with her hands in front of Darcy's mother's face. "She's not a serious rider. She's a kid having fun. And *you* are a nuisance. I'd like you to leave. Now."

Darcy held her breath. Her mother stared at Ms. Blakely, her eyes narrowed and one nail tapping against her leg.

"I'll go," she said. "Straight to the headmistress to ask for your dismissal." She looked over at Darcy. "I'll see you Saturday.

Maybe you'll do better then." She looked at Dusty with a sneer on her face. "Of course, if that glue factory reject is the best they can do here, I doubt you'll ever really learn to ride." Then she turned on her heel and walked back into the barn. In the next minute, a motor roared and tires squealed.

When Darcy looked back at Ms. Blakely, the trainer stood with her hands on her hips, her head hanging forward onto her chest.

"I'm sorry," Darcy said quietly. "I didn't ask her to come."

"I know." Ms. Blakely sighed and lifted her chin. "I tried to hold on to my temper."

"She can be really hard to take." Darcy slid out of the saddle. "Will she get you fired?"

"Not likely. Ms. Thomas knows the story about your mother." She put a hand on Darcy's shoulder. "Today was rough, but you held it together. Do the same thing Saturday and you'll be just fine."

Darcy looked around as she led Dusty toward the barn. Eve sat inside the pasture fence with Snowflake, brushing the mini-horse's white tail. Snowflake looked totally relaxed, and Eve had a soft smile on her face.

At least *someone* was having a good afternoon.

AFTER A full day's work on Friday, Ruth Ann finally allowed Jonah to walk her to her cottage about eleven o'clock, when she couldn't think of any details they hadn't triple-checked in the last few hours. He gave her warm, comforting kisses and a long hug before ordering her into bed.

She doubted she'd be able to sleep, even though her body ached and she felt as if a knife had been driven into her head between her eyes. There were still so many details she wasn't sure she'd planned properly. They would torture her all night.

She'd just changed into her comfortably worn green flannel pajamas when the doorbell rang. Even for Jonah, she decided, she wasn't going to make the effort to change again. She pulled on an equally threadbare purple robe, then went to the door.

Her anticipation evaporated when she saw Brittany standing on her front porch. She didn't have the energy to be polite. "What do you want?"

"We need to talk." Brittany stalked past her into the house.

"No, we do not need to talk. I'm exhausted. Leave, please."

"Not before I warn you."

Ruth Ann held up a hand. "Oh, give me a break. Did you come over here to tell me Jonah's just using me to make sure the new stable contract is approved? Don't quit your day job to start writing books, Brittany. That plot is as clichéd as they come."

"I think that's exactly what he's doing. Because he used me the same way."

"Brittany—"

"I had only been widowed a year when I ended up working on the interior of a barn Jonah was designing."

"Yes, I know."

"I didn't want to date, let alone start another relationship." She sighed. "But Jonah was so charming, so handsome, so... persuasive." She brushed the bangs out of her eyes. "And still is. I was planning to arrive in Ridgeville tonight, watch the show tomorrow and leave again on Sunday, but he convinced me to take a few days off so we could get together, have a chance to relax and really talk. We had a lovely dinner together last night."

"Sure." Arms crossed over her chest, Ruth Ann called up the biggest sneer she possessed. Of course, Jonah had told her he'd met Brittany for dinner. To keep her out of trouble, he said.

"When we were working together, he would flirt with me, touching me and giving me that terrific smile of his, and I couldn't help falling for him. What I didn't realize was that he knew I was friends with Stephen Julian, and he wanted me to introduce them."

Despite a small prickle of doubt, Ruth Ann maintained her skepticism. "I don't care about your history with Jonah. Please let me go to sleep." She was feeling less and less desirable, standing here with dirty hair, in her ratty flannel pajamas, while Brittany lounged on the sofa in a chic knit dress and high-heeled boots with pointed toes.

"I did introduce them, and I watched him using the same seduction techniques with Stephen that he'd used on me."

"Jonah is a nice guy. People like him. That's not calculation."

"Perhaps. But when I asked him to marry me, after he signed the contract with Stephen, he said he didn't have any use for me any more—until I told him I was pregnant with his baby."

A terrible pain exploded in Ruth Ann's chest. She didn't have the strength to say a word.

"It was true," Brittany assured her. "But after the wedding, I lost the baby."

Ruth Ann recovered some of her control. "And then, of course, Jonah treated you badly until you finally divorced him?" Her voice was shaky, breathless.

"No, he tried to make the best of a bad situation, I think. He did like my money—he used it to buy into Stephen's firm." These lies skimmed too close to the truth. At this point, Ruth Ann wasn't sure of the difference.

"I couldn't give Jonah enough money to buy a rug for his new house. So there's nothing to worry about." She marched to the door and opened it. "Now, please, get out."

Brittany did, at last, come up off the couch. "He needs this project, you know. Desperately. If he loses the Hawkridge contract, he won't be able to maintain his own firm. He's already severed his ties with Stephen, so he'll be out of a job. And I don't plan to pay Darcy's school fees." She shrugged. "I guess she'll be stuck going to Hickville public schools."

She glanced at Ruth Ann as she sashayed over the threshold. "He's very clever. I suspect he knew your opposition would make Miriam Edwards and her Board of Directors more determined to proceed. All Jonah had to do was spur you a little in the direction you already wanted to go. A technique that works with horses and stubborn people." She waved a hand over her shoulder. "Good night. See you at the show tomorrow."

The windows rattled when Ruth Ann slammed the door. She stomped through the house, turning off lights, and then climbed into bed.

Sleep evaded her, and she spent the night going over Brittany's and Jonah's stories—noting the similarities, which were many, and the differences, which were crucial. She wanted to believe Jonah. She believed him.

And yet, she'd always doubted a man like Jonah would spend his life with a woman like her. He hadn't told her about the house he'd bought in Ridgeville until she'd asked, and he hadn't told her about Brittany's poor baby. If he cared, surely he would have been more open about his past, let alone his present and his future.

Even after sex, when they lay wrapped around each other, as close as two humans could get, Jonah hadn't suggested making plans. Maybe she'd been useful, Ruth Ann decided. He'd been attracted to her, maybe because she'd kept him at a distance longer than most women did. But there had never been a real chance that getting close to him would bring her anything but pain.

Just because she'd fallen in love with Jonah Granger didn't mean he could have fallen in love with her.

Chapter Fourteen

The Hawkridge School Horse Show proved to be a resounding success. Ruth Ann opened the day with a performance of Waldo's freestyle dressage routine, which drew sounds of amazement from the spectators and, at the end, a huge standing ovation. Jonah mingled with the crowd as the competition classes commenced, listening to comments, scouting potential problems, assessing the reactions of participants and spectators alike.

He had no trouble reading the moods of the riders—the girls from Hawkridge were all having the best day of their lives, whether working as volunteers, sprucing up their horses before a class, or riding in the class itself. Some of them won ribbons, which were presented immediately following the judge's assessment of each group, and some didn't. But they came into the barn smiling either way.

The students from nearby schools, who had brought their own horses with them, seemed to be having an equally good time. Jonah made a point of introducing himself to the trainers and coaches from the other schools, and found them enthusiastic and complimentary about every aspect of Ruth Ann's show.

He looked for her to tell her so, but he could never track

her down. Everywhere he thought she might be, she had just left. No one seemed to know where she would appear next.

Darcy and Dusty were showing in two classes, the first to start at ten o'clock. While searching for a place from which to observe his stepdaughter's success, Jonah responded to a wave from Jayne Thomas and went to sit beside the headmistress on one of the lower bleachers near the center of the arena.

A minute later, Brittany plopped herself down on Jayne's other side.

"This is so exciting." She wore the fur-trimmed coat again, over black jeans and a bright-red sweater. "I hope Darcy manages to stay on."

"I'm sure she will," Jayne said. "Ruth Ann has told me about the progress she's made with her riding."

"Well, the lesson I observed Thursday didn't impress me, as I told you that afternoon." Brittany smoothed the leather gloves covering her fingers. "Have you considered my suggestion?"

Jonah leaned forward. "What suggestion?"

Jayne's face remained calm and pleasant. "No, I'm afraid I didn't consider your suggestion. I have no intention of firing Ruth Ann Blakely. She's too valuable to the school as a therapist and teacher."

Jonah clenched his hands on his knees. "You thought you could get away with that?"

Brittany's lower lip stuck out in a pout. "She was rude. Insubordinate. And she clearly doesn't have a clue about how to teach a child to ride."

At that moment, the announcer summoned Darcy and the rest of the riders in the Walk/Trot class into the arena. Twelve horses entered the gate and began to walk along the arena fence.

"She looks great." Dismissing Brittany with a shrug, Jonah

watched his stepdaughter and grinned in pride. "Like she belongs on the horse."

Jayne nodded. "She's relaxed and confident."

Brittany sniffed.

The horses in the class ranged from Dusty, the palomino pony, to a tall chestnut thoroughbred whose rider couldn't keep him going in a straight line. They all walked one way, turned and went the other direction, and then repeated the exercise at a trot. To finish, the class was asked to line up in the center of the arena, facing the judge.

The ribbons were awarded in reverse order, starting with sixth place.

Third place went to another girl from Hawkridge, and Brittany stirred. "Well, Darcy can't possibly have come in higher than third. As I said—"

The second-place rider was a boy from the nearby military school. Then the announcer said, "And the blue ribbon goes to the winner of the Walk/Trot class—Darcy Granger on Dusty!"

A cheer went up from the Hawkridge girls standing around the arena, adding to the applause of the crowd as Darcy urged Dusty forward to accept her ribbon. The bright smile on her face brought tears to Jonah's eyes.

Her next class, Go As You Please, followed immediately, so Darcy didn't leave the arena. She handed her ribbon to Eve, who seemed to be waiting near the gate for just that purpose.

"Now what does that mean, Go As You Please?" Jayne Thomas asked. Jonah started to answer, but Brittany took over.

"The judge will ask for the walk and trot, just as before, but then she'll announce 'Go as you please' and the riders are allowed to choose which gait they'll display. If the horse has a fantastic trot—which Darcy's doesn't—then the rider might choose to display the trot. Most riders go for the canter, because horses generally look good cantering and it's a more advanced skill." She shook her head. "I hope Darcy chooses to trot. She won't be scored at all if she falls off."

Many of the same horses and riders participating in this class had been in the last one. The thoroughbred, settled down now that he was used to the arena, preferred to canter and his rider allowed him that freedom. A few of the younger riders trotted, but most horses also went into a canter at the Go-As-You-Please signal.

Jonah switched his attention to Darcy at the very moment she decided to canter. He saw the deep breath she took, and the slight flick of her whip. Dusty lifted up in front, and, to Jonah's surprise, moved smoothly into an easy canter, with Darcy looking competent, if not completely relaxed, in the saddle. When asked to trot again, they did so without incident, turned, and cantered in the opposite direction as if they'd been together for years.

No falls for Darcy. Whatever ribbon she got for this ride, she and Ruth Ann both came out looking like winners.

Jonah glanced over at Brittany. "That went pretty well." He didn't have to say anything else. She got the point.

"Yes," she said in a tight voice, "it did."

The thoroughbred earned the blue ribbon this time, with his long, elegant stride and graceful style. Darcy and Dusty came in third place, which was just fine with Jonah. There would always be room for improvement.

Jayne Thomas congratulated both of them, and left the stands to mingle with the board members in the special tent set up for their use. Jonah promised her he would be along to join her in a few minutes. First, he wanted to talk to Darcy. And, with luck, Ruth Ann.

Brittany caught his hand as he stood up. "You think you've won, don't you?"

To keep the conversation as quiet as possible, Jonah sat down again. "What are you talking about?"

"You brought Darcy here, and now you think you've won because she's earned a couple of ribbons at a two-bit show."

He sighed. "Believe it or not, Brittany, I'm not out to win anything. I just want Darcy to be happy, to feel good about herself. She never did that with you. And I want a home I can share with her. I don't wish anything bad for you. I just want you to go away and leave us alone."

She lifted one eyebrow. "Oh, I'll leave you alone. Very much alone." This time, she was the one who stood up. "Ta-ta."

Jonah understood the menace in her words. He couldn't quite imagine what she might have done to hurt him.

He found out about eight o'clock that night, after all the visitors had left, after the girls and their parents had gone back to the dorm to get luggage for the week-long Thanksgiving vacation, after the horses were fed and bedded down, and Hector and Ruben had been given bonuses for their work above and beyond the call of duty. Once Ruth Ann couldn't find a single task to do that would keep her busy and out of sight, Jonah discovered what Brittany had done.

He stood motionless for a minute or more after Ruth Ann described his ex-wife's Friday-night visit, her depiction of their relationship. He didn't have much trouble believing Brittany would try to pull a stunt like this.

"I told you what happened," he said, when he thought he could control his voice.

"You didn't say you'd married her because she was pregnant."

Jonah swallowed hard. "I would have married her anyway. But, yes. There was a baby. He died."

"Why did you leave that part out?" Her green eyes were wide with hurt.

"I don't know!" He put up his hands in a helpless gesture. "Because I don't like thinking about it, maybe. Because I'm sorry that our marriage happened like that. To shield Brittany, I guess, though for the life of me I don't know why I'd want to."

"Did you think you could use me to finesse the Hawkridge stable contract?"

"I want to design a building that's both beautiful and functional. I want you to help me do exactly that."

"You need this contract to build a business here. Darcy's recovery and your career depend on the Hawkridge stable. You needed to be sure."

"Yes, but that hasn't got anything to do with you. Us."

He came across the lounge and took hold of her shoulders. "Why don't you trust me? Why would you believe Brittany, instead?"

"Because it's too much…too much of a fairytale." Ruth Ann moved away from his touch. "You and me. We're nothing alike, have nothing in common."

Like her parents. All of a sudden, Jonah understood. And with understanding came exhaustion. He nearly staggered under the weight of his own bones and muscles.

"You let Brittany play you," he said, backing up. "You took the opportunity she gave you to return to that safe place you've made for yourself—the place where you're alone with your horses and you don't have to worry about taking any risks. You don't have to change and you don't have to try."

He turned and went to the door. "I love you, Ruth Ann. I guess I could prove it to you by throwing away the Hawkridge contract, but you're right—I need the money. More than that, I need a woman who trusts me, who's willing to risk everything to be with me. I'm not interested in a one-sided relationship. If you want me, you're going to have to reach out and grab me."

Jonah regretted the words almost as soon as he said them. Ruth Ann was just stubborn enough to ignore her own heart, and his, because she didn't believe in happy endings.

He might very well spend the rest of his life wishing he'd simply kept his mouth shut.

WITH MOST of the girls off-campus for the holiday, Ruth Ann spent more time in her cottage than at the barn. She unplugged the answering machine and the phone, didn't check her mail on the computer. The television stayed on, but she slept through most of the programs. She tried not to think about anything at all.

Monday morning dawned clear, but by noon the wind had freshened and storm clouds began piling up against the mountains. A giant thunderclap woke Ruth Ann at two o'clock. She sat up on the couch, raking her hands through her hair and thinking she might need to check on the horses. Some of them got a little spooked during storms.

This storm broke while she was slowly pulling herself together. Slashing rain and shrieking wind joined the flash and crash of lightning and thunder. Only a fool—or someone who worried about vulnerable friends—would venture out if they didn't have to.

The fiasco with Jonah had proven to Ruth Ann that she was nothing if not a fool.

Wearing rubber boots and a raincoat with the hood pulled up, she left through her kitchen door and headed for the barn. Gusts of wind battered her, strong enough to shift her direction several times before she reached the shelter of the trees.

Only a few feet into the woods, she saw someone running toward her on the path. "Eve? What are you doing out—"

The girl ran right into her, grabbed her hand and reversed direction, pulling hard. "A tree fell," she said, panting. "On the stable. There were…" She dragged in another breath. "…sparks."

Ruth Ann started running, too. While still in the woods, she could hear the horses screaming. When she and Eve reached the barn, she saw flames.

A pine tree in the parking area—probably one of the oldest trees left standing around the barn—now lay across the front part of the roof. A charred stripe edged with fire spiraled down the trunk, indicating a lightning strike.

Underneath the tree, the siding had started to burn.

Ruth Ann grabbed Eve by the shoulders. "We have to get the horses out. Can you help me?"

Eyes big in her thin face, Eve nodded.

"Good. I'll put their halters on. You have to take them out to the field."

They started on the stalls behind the lounge, because the flames were closer there. Smoke filled the aisle, and the horses had begun to panic. With her lack of experience, Eve could barely manage the smaller horses and ponies. What would happen when they got to the big guys?

By the time they reached the end of the aisle, flames had started to lick at the stalls themselves. And there were still five horses to go on the other side.

"How can I help?"

She whirled and saw Jonah standing in the smoky rain. No time to ask why he'd come. "Help me get the rest of the horses."

They sent Eve to stand with Darcy by the pasture gate. Jonah didn't argue when Ruth Ann insisted on staying in the barn while he took the animals out. These five were her most temperamental—if she couldn't get them haltered, no one could.

And each horse was just about as wild as he could be in the confines of a stall. She got kicked and stepped on, more than once. Head high, nostrils flaring and eyes showing white, Excel nearly killed her before she got his halter on.

But Jonah waited without comment, took the rope when she handed it over and led the fearful horse away so she could go on to repeat the experience with Ruffian.

The last horse on the aisle was Dusty. "Darcy and I got him," Jonah said, when Ruth Ann reached that point. He grabbed her hand. "You're done. Come on."

She followed him out of the thick black smoke to the pasture, where she counted twice to be sure all the horses were present. Eve and Darcy huddled together by the fence, staring at her with wide, fearful eyes. Sirens sounded in the distance— Jonah had called the fire department with his cell phone.

"Thank you so much." Ruth Ann put her arms around the two girls at the same time. "Eve, I don't know what I would have done without you." She kissed the top of her wet blond head. "And Darcy, I'm so glad you got Dusty out for me. I was running out of time and strength." Hugging them both close, she squeezed her eyes against the tears waiting to fall. The horses. The girls. Jonah and herself. Everyone and everything that mattered was safe.

Then she turned around to look at the barn. Her barn, now blazing like a bonfire. As she watched, the pine tree broke into two pieces. The roof underneath the pieces collapsed, and a huge fountain of flames and sparks erupted. In the field behind Ruth Ann, the horses whinnied and wheeled away, racing toward the far fence to watch from a place of safety.

She realized she was holding the girls too tightly, and

loosened her arms. "Why don't you two go up to my cottage and get dry?" The rain had turned to drizzle, and had no effect on the burning wood.

"Why don't you go with them?" Jonah stood in front of her, blocking the view. "There's no reason to stand here and watch, is there? Take Darcy and Eve, get some dry clothes on and something warm to drink. I'll come along in a while."

Ruth Ann looked up at him, saw nothing but sadness and concern for her in his face. He wanted to share her burden.

And she wanted him to.

With a last glance at the fire, Ruth Ann turned herself and the two girls away.

An hour later, as they sat at her dining room table drinking hot chocolate, a question occurred to Ruth Ann.

"What were you two doing at the barn, anyway?" She looked from Eve to Darcy and back again. "Didn't you go home for the vacation?"

Eve shook her head. "My mom went to Aspen to ski with her boyfriend. I was out running and thought I'd go by to see Snowflake. Then the storm started, and the tree got hit by that first huge lightning strike. It was crazy loud. I saw the sparks, and came for you."

"Thank God," Ruth Ann said fervently. "And thank you."

Eve blushed and hid her face by taking a long sip of her hot chocolate.

"Jonah and I were here to get Eve to come home with us," Darcy said. "When she wasn't in the room, I thought she might be at the barn." She gave a shy smile. "And I wanted to see Dusty. So we drove over, but—" The smile vanished. "I'm so sorry."

"The horses are safe. That's what matters." Ruth Ann would keep telling herself that, until she was alone, at least.

They all drank in silence for a few minutes, occasionally

munching on the gingersnap cookies Ruth Ann had found in her cupboard.

Then Darcy stirred in her chair. "What do you do on Thanksgiving? Do you go somewhere for dinner?"

Ruth Ann grinned, remembering. "I have my Thanksgiving with the horses—I feed them all apples as a treat and save one for myself." A vision flashed through her mind of how immensely complicated feeding the horses would be now, with no barn and all her hay and grain and buckets burned to ashes. Not to mention the saddles, the bridles, the blankets…

She forced her mind to go blank, a skill she'd been practicing frequently these last few days. "I usually eat dinner in the dining hall with Ms. Thomas and the girls who have stayed."

"Could you eat with us?" Darcy glanced at her roommate. "Eve's coming home with me today. We're going to cook a big turkey and make pies and mashed potatoes and everything." She grinned. 'I'll have to shovel all the stalls—" Her eyes widened, filled with tears. "I forgot," she whispered.

"It's okay." Ruth Ann gave her shoulders a squeeze. "Believe me, with so many horses on the grass, the Manure Diet is in full effect. We'll have to clean up or the fields will be seas of horse poop.' She took a deep breath. "I really don't think I'll be good company for Thanksgiving, though I do appreciate the invitation."

"Please? Oh, please?" The next thing she knew, both Eve and Darcy were pestering her, teasing her, badgering her to come to Jonah's house for Thanksgiving dinner. And though it all seemed like joking, Ruth Ann understood this was important to both girls. After what they'd done for her today, disappointing them would just be plain mean.

"Okay, okay, I'll be there. Can I bring something?" What, she didn't know. Her cooking skills were minimal.

The girls brushed away her offer of a contribution. Finishing their hot chocolate, they started making up the menu, which soon became so large and complicated that Ruth Ann suggested they invite the whole town. She liked the idea—she'd have an easier time of hiding from Jonah that way.

When he finally walked through her kitchen door, wearing soot all over his clothes, face and hands, his expression was grim. "The fire chief would like to talk to you down at the stable."

"They're not finished?"

He shook his head. "They'll be a long time yet, making sure everything's out." His hand came up, as if he wanted to touch her, but then fell back to his side. "I'm sorry, Ruth Ann. I wouldn't have had this happen for anything."

"I know." They stood together for a moment, with the girls' laughter in the background. What she wanted, more than anything, was to rest her head against his strong chest and cry. Instead, she straightened her back and lifted her chin. "Darcy invited me for Thanksgiving dinner. I told her I would come, but if you would rather—"

His lips curved into a smile. "That's great. I told her she could ask. Does two o'clock on Thursday work for you?"

"Um…sure." She hadn't expected him to know about the invitation. He wanted her to come to his house? What did that mean?

When she looked at him, the smile had become a grin. "Don't think too much, or too hard. You've got other stuff to worry about. I'll get the girls out of your way so you can go talk to the fire department." Then he did touch her face with his fingertips, briefly. "See you Thursday."

For the first time in days—in years?—Ruth Ann felt free to breathe.

Going back to the barn was a test of her fortitude, but the fire chief and his crews made the post mortem as easy as possible for her. She started wondering, late in the afternoon, what she would feed the horses for dinner—the grass in the pasture had gone dormant for the winter, and would never sustain so many animals, even at its greenest.

The fire trucks had barely driven off, however, when three more trucks came up the service road, two of them loaded down with hay. In a few minutes, men from the neighboring farms had erected a sturdy tarp and put down wooden pallets underneath so they could unload hay bales. The nearby military school had sent twenty bags of feed and twenty buckets for her horses to eat out of.

Dinner was served.

On Tuesday and Wednesday, Ruth Ann received even more help from people in the area, as well as from the schools that had sent riders to the Hawkridge show—more hay and feed and blankets, the promise of saddles and tack when she needed them, and a gift of new bits from the local feed store. Mr. Harris at the hardware store sent a storage building to protect all the equipment. Miriam Edwards personally delivered an expensive feed supplement Ruth Ann liked to use but couldn't, at this moment, afford to buy.

"I'm sorry," the older woman said as she gazed at the ashes. "I would never have chosen to burn down your barn as a way to make room for a new one."

"I know." Ruth Ann kept her gaze on the horses in the field. "It's okay." Miriam gave her a hug and left with tears in her eyes.

Ruth Ann couldn't believe she and Miriam had reached a state of friendship. If that minor miracle had come true, what else should she try to believe?

Chapter Fifteen

The bell on Jonah's front door rang at one forty-five. In the kitchen, Darcy looked at Eve. "That's her!"

Eve grinned. "Do you think he's going to ask her today?"

Darcy put the pot lid over the cooked potatoes. "I hope so. You heard him last night—walking up and down the floor until practically daylight. Won't that be cool—my dad and Ms. Blakely? I hope she'll let us be bridesmaids!"

Another ring was followed by Jonah's call from the second floor. "Are you getting that, Darcy? You said you wanted to."

"We're coming, we're coming." She and Eve ran through the house and Darcy flung the door back. "Come in, come in. Did you know it's supposed to snow today?"

Ms. Blakely smiled at them, her cheeks flushed a pretty pink. "I did hear that." She looked beautiful, with her shiny hair loose around her shoulders. Darcy had never seen her so dressed up, except when she wore her dressage coat. Today's orange sweater and brown corduroy pants looked even better.

"We made real cranberry sauce," Eve declared. "Out of real cranberries and everything!"

"Sounds delicious. I love cranberries and cranberry sauce." Ms. Blakely looked up at Jonah, who had come halfway down the stairs. "Hi. Thanks for having me. I brought some wine." Holding up the bottle, she grinned at his raised eyebrow. "I got it from Jayne. She said it would be very good."

Jonah came down to the floor and took the bottle, glancing at the label. The expression on his face reminded Darcy of a little kid on Christmas morning. She didn't think it was because of the wine.

"Yes," he said, "that'll be terrific." He handed the wine to Darcy. "Could you put this in the fridge?"

She started to protest, then remembered the plan and hustled away. After a minute in the kitchen, she returned with a mug of the spiced cider she and Eve had warmed up.

"Delicious," Ms. Blakely declared. "The perfect taste for Thanksgiving Day. Can I see what you're cooking?" She glanced at Jonah, her gaze shy. "And I'd like to tour the house, too."

"That's all on the program." He gave Darcy a pointed look, and she nodded. "I have something I'd like to show you first. This way." He beckoned to Ms. Blakely and turned around to go up the steps.

As they disappeared on the second floor, Darcy turned to Eve. "He's going to do it," she whispered, jumping up and down. "He's really going to ask her! Awesome!"

AT THE TOP of the staircase, Jonah turned right. Ruth Ann followed him down the long, wide hallway, listening to their footsteps on the polished floorboards.

The room he entered seemed very bright compared to the dim hallway. Stepping in after him, Ruth Ann saw tracklighting had been strategically arranged to highlight easels set up around the walls.

"Is this where you work?" A big desk and bookcases occupied one wall that wasn't filled with windows. "It's gorg—"

Then she recognized the drawings on the easels. "Jonah? What is this?"

He indicated the book on the drawing table. "It starts there."

With her stomach fluttering like a flock of butterflies and a huge lump in her throat, Ruth Ann went to the high, wide work surface. The book lying on top was eighteen inches high and two feet wide when open, with onionskin pages and old-fashioned type. Before concentrating on the pages Jonah wanted her to see, she folded the front cover over. The red leather binding had been stamped and embossed with gold lettering—*Architectural Plans and Descriptions for Buildings on the Hawkridge Estate.*

She looked up at Jonah. He tilted his head. "Go on."

The pages he'd revealed showed the original design for the Hawkridge Stable. "This is wonderful," she murmured. "I had no idea." Her chest hurt and her eyes teared up as she gazed at the drawings of her barn as it had once stood. And was no more.

After paging through the chapters on the stable, she straightened up and took a deep breath. "That's wonderful, Jonah. How did you find the book? I didn't know something like this existed."

"I wasn't sure, but I thought it was worth a try. The Hawkridge librarian showed me all the documentation on the construction of the estate—which would also make a terrific book someday—and there was this volume, just waiting to be discovered."

With reverence, Ruth Ann closed the giant cover. "Thanks for showing me. I'm glad to know—"

But Jonah was shaking his head. "That's not all, Ruth Ann. The rest of the project is here." He gestured toward the easels.

He wanted her to consider his design again, even though

it had already been approved by the board. At the very least, she owed him for helping her during the fire. Walking over to the nearest easel, she resolved to be honest, but encouraging.

When she looked at the first drawing, however, she found herself speechless. Moving to the second, the third and fourth, she couldn't voice a single word. There were twelve pictures, all of them showing different aspects of a barn that looked very much like hers—only better. Newer, with modern materials and fixtures that could only make life easier Updated, as well, with contemporary details which undeniably improved the overall design. Despite all the changes, however, this was essentially the same barn she'd worked in her entire life.

"I don't understand." Ruth Ann turned to Jonah. "You couldn't possibly have done this just since Monday."

He shook his head. "More like the last six weeks. I realized the only hope of getting you to agree would be to give you a new barn as much like your old one as possible. So I found the plan and tried to bring it into the twenty-first century. It may still need some work, but—"

"No, oh, no." She faced the drawings and plans again. "It's wonderful!" The tears she hadn't given into in the last week wouldn't be restrained. And she couldn't seem to wipe them away fast enough.

"Ruth Ann." His warm, caring voice came from just behind her. The heat from his body reached out to her. With a sob, she jerked around and huddled against Jonah's chest, just as his arms reached out to hold her there.

She didn't know how long she cried. When she finally caught her breath, she and Jonah were seated on the big, black leather sofa in the bay window, with her knees against the back of the seat so she could stay cuddled against him.

"I'm sorry." He kissed her temples, her cheekbones, her forehead and nose. "I'm so sorry you lost your barn."

Ruth Ann sniffed and sighed. "Me, too."

"I had an idea, though." He stroked her hair back off her wet face. "The stones and bricks won't have burned. We can clean them up and incorporate them into the new building. We'll have the old and the new joined together that way."

Her tears overflowed once again. And again he held her, stroking and soothing, until the grief subsided.

"So," he said when she drew back a little, "do you think you could stay at Hawkridge if you had to work out of this barn?"

Ruth Ann played with his shirt button. "What about Miriam and her German trainer?"

"I told her before the show that I'd withdraw my plan for the project if she tried to force you out of the job."

"You did what?" She stared at him. "What about your business? You need the contract!"

"But I need you more."

The simple declaration left her breathless. "Do you really think—" She stopped, considering what she'd been about to say.

Jonah watched her, his brows drawn together. "Do I think what?"

Ruth Ann took a deep breath and blew it out again. "You know, I'm not going to ask that question. Instead, I'm going to say this—I need you, too, Jonah." She smiled as his frown eased and a grin began to emerge. "And I think we'll be terrific together, because we are different enough to be interesting, but we care enough to make compromises."

"That's some change of heart." He held her with one hand, while the fingers of the other hand played around the V-neck of her sweater. "I like the way you're thinking, Ms. Blakely."

"Make that Ruth Ann," she said. "We can't do this properly unless we're on a first-name basis." With an arm around his neck, she brought his face to hers for a kiss of passion and commitment.

Jonah drew back far sooner than she wanted him to. "You are going to marry me, right? I just want to be sure I have all the details straight. Before Christmas?" He bent his head for another deep kiss. "I really don't want to wait too long to start my life with you. I love you, Ruth Ann. Everything about you."

Married. Did she dare? Could she bear not to?

"I love you, too." She kissed him with all of her heart and soul on her lips. "I'm thrilled to marry you."

Just as Jonah slid his hand under her sweater, footsteps stomped up the stairs. "Jonah? The turkey's gonna burn unless you take it out. And we have to mash the potatoes."

Ruth Ann grinned and sat up away from him. "Duty calls." Then, glancing out the window, she gasped. "It *is* snowing!"

He turned to watch, and slipped his arm around her. "Nice. My first Smoky Mountain snow."

"There will be many more," Ruth Ann promised him. "This is your home." She sighed. "And mine."

"Ours." He bent his head for a kiss.

"Jonah!" Darcy's voice came from the doorway. "I'm gonna remind you of this when you give me a hard time about my boyfriends. Come down to the kitchen. Now."

"Bossy women," he murmured, bringing Ruth Ann with him as he left the room. "Whatever happened to honor and *obey?*"

"Obey? Hah!" Ruth Ann laughed, looking forward to a bright and loving future. "Have you got a surprise in store!"

* * * * *

Turn the page for a sneak preview of
AFTERSHOCK, *a new anthology*
featuring New York Times *bestselling author*
Sharon Sala.

Available October 2008.

nocturne™

Dramatic and sensual tales of paranormal romance.

Chapter 1

October
New York City

Nicole Masters was sitting cross-legged on her sofa while a cold autumn rain peppered the windows of her fourth-floor apartment. She was poking at the ice cream in her bowl and trying not to be in a mood.

Six weeks ago, a simple trip to her neighborhood pharmacy had turned into a nightmare. She'd walked into the middle of a robbery. She never even saw the man who shot her in the head and left her for dead. She'd survived, but some of her senses had not. She was dealing with short-term memory loss and a tendency to stagger. Even though she'd been told the problems were most likely temporary, she waged a daily battle with depression.

Her parents had been killed in a car wreck when she was

twenty-one. And except for a few friends—and most recently her boyfriend, Dominic Tucci, who lived in the apartment right above hers, she was alone. Her doctor kept reminding her that she should be grateful to be alive, and on one level she knew he was right. But he wasn't living in her shoes.

If she'd been anywhere else but at that pharmacy when the robbery happened, she wouldn't have died twice on the way to the hospital. Instead of being grateful that she'd survived, she couldn't stop thinking of what she'd lost.

But that wasn't the end of her troubles. On top of everything else, something strange was happening inside her head. She'd begun to hear odd things: sounds, not voices—at least, she didn't think it was voices. It was more like the distant noise of rapids—a rush of wind and water inside her head that, when it came, blocked out everything around her. It didn't happen often, but when it did, it was frightening, and it was driving her crazy.

The blank moments, which is what she called them, even had a rhythm. First there came that sound, then a cold sweat, then panic with no reason. Part of her feared it was the beginning of an emotional breakdown. And part of her feared it wasn't—that it was going to turn out to be a permanent souvenir of her resurrection.

Frustrated with herself and the situation as it stood, she upped the sound on the TV remote. But instead of *Wheel of Fortune,* an announcer broke in with a special bulletin.

"This just in. Police are on the scene of a kidnapping that occurred only hours ago at The Dakota. Molly Dane, the six-year-old daughter of one of Hollywood's block-buster stars, Lyla Dane, was taken by force from the family apartment. At this time they have yet to receive a ransom demand. The housekeeper was seriously injured during the abduction, and is, at the present time, in surgery. Police are hoping to be able to talk to her once she regains consciousness. In the meantime, we are going now to a press conference with Lyla Dane."

Horrified, Nicole stilled as the cameras went live to where the actress was speaking before a bank of microphones. The shock and terror in Lyla Dane's voice were physically painful to watch. But even though Nicole kept upping the volume, the sound continued to fade.

Just when she was beginning to think something was wrong with her set, the broadcast suddenly switched from the Dane press conference to what appeared to be footage of the kidnapping, beginning with footage from inside the apartment.

When the front door suddenly flew back against the wall and four men rushed in, Nicole gasped. Horrified, she quickly realized that this must have been caught on a security camera inside the Dane apartment.

As Nicole continued to watch, a small Asian woman, who she guessed was the maid, rushed forward in an effort to keep them out. When one of the men hit her in the face with his gun, Nicole moaned. The violence was too reminiscent of what she'd lived through. Sick to her stomach, she fisted her hands against her belly, wishing it was over, but unable to tear her gaze away.

When the maid dropped to the carpet, the same man followed with a vicious kick to the little woman's midsection that lifted her off the floor.

"Oh, my God," Nicole said. When blood began to pool beneath the maid's head, she started to cry.

As the tape played on, the four men split up in different directions. The camera caught one running down a long marble hallway, then disappearing into a room. Moments later he reappeared, carrying a little girl, who Nicole assumed was Molly Dane. The child was wearing a pair of red pants and a white turtleneck sweater, and her hair was partially blocking her abductor's face as he carried her down the hall. She was kicking and screaming in his arms, and when he slapped her, it elicited an agonized scream that brought the other three running. Nicole watched in horror as one of them ran up and put his hand over Molly's face. Seconds later, she went limp.

One moment they were in the foyer, then they were gone.

Nicole jumped to her feet, then staggered drunkenly. The bowl of ice cream she'd absentmindedly placed in her lap shattered at her feet, splattering glass and melting ice cream everywhere.

The picture on the screen abruptly switched from the kidnapping to what Nicole assumed was a rerun of Lyla Dane's plea for her daughter's safe return, but she was numb.

Before she could think what to do next, the doorbell rang. Startled by the unexpected sound, she shakily swiped at the tears and took a step forward. She didn't feel the glass shards piercing her feet until she took the second step. At that point, sharp pains shot through her foot. She gasped, then looked down in confusion. Her legs looked as if she'd been running through mud, and she was standing in broken glass and ice cream, while a thin ribbon of blood seeped out from beneath her toes.

"Oh, no," Nicole mumbled, then stifled a second moan of pain.

The doorbell rang again. She shivered, then clutched her head in confusion.

"Just a minute!" she yelled, then tried to sidestep the rest of the debris as she hobbled to the door.

When she looked through the peephole in the door, she didn't know whether to be relieved or regretful.

It was Dominic, and as usual, she was a mess.

Nicole smiled a little self-consciously as she opened the door to let him in. "I just don't know what's happening to me. I think I'm losing my mind."

"Hey, don't talk about my woman like that."

Nicole rode the surge of delight his words brought. "So I'm still your woman?"

Dominic lowered his head.

Their lips met.

The kiss proceeded.

Slowly.

Thoroughly.

* * * * *

Be sure to look for the
AFTERSHOCK *anthology next month,*
as well as other exciting paranormal stories
from Silhouette Nocturne.
Available in October
wherever books are sold.

Silhouette®

nocturne™

NEW YORK TIMES BESTSELLING AUTHOR

SHARON SALA

JANIS REAMES HUDSON
DEBRA COWAN

AFTERSHOCK

Three women are brought to the brink of death…
only to discover the aftershock of their trauma has
left them with unexpected and unwelcome gifts of
paranormal powers. Now each woman must learn to
accept her newfound abilities while fighting for life,
love and second chances….

Available October wherever books are sold.

www.eHarlequin.com
www.paranormalromanceblog.wordpress.com   SN61796

SILHOUETTE

SPECIAL EDITION™

BRAVO FAMILY TIES

Tanner Bravo and Crystal Cerise had it bad
for each other, though they couldn't be more
different. Tanner was the type to settle down;
free-spirited Crystal wouldn't hear of it.
Now that Crystal was pregnant, would
Tanner have his way after all?

Look for

HAVING
TANNER BRAVO'S
BABY

by *USA TODAY* bestselling author
CHRISTINE RIMMER

Available in October wherever books are sold.

REQUEST YOUR FREE BOOKS!
2 FREE NOVELS PLUS 2
FREE GIFTS!

Heart, Home & Happiness!

YES! Please send me 2 FREE Harlequin American Romance® novels and my 2 FREE gifts (gifts are worth about $10). After receiving them, if I don't wish to receive any more books, I can return the shipping statement marked "cancel." If I don't cancel, I will receive 4 brand-new novels every month and be billed just $4.24 per book in the U.S. or $4.99 per book in Canada, plus 25¢ shipping and handling per book and applicable taxes, if any*. That's a savings of close to 15% off the cover price! I understand that accepting the 2 free books and gifts places me under no obligation to buy anything. I can always return a shipment and cancel at any time. Even if I never buy another book from Harlequin, the two free books and gifts are mine to keep forever.

154 HDN EEZK 354 HDN EEZV

Name	(PLEASE PRINT)	
Address		Apt. #
City	State/Prov.	Zip/Postal Code

Signature (if under 18, a parent or guardian must sign)

Mail to the **Harlequin Reader Service:**
IN U.S.A.: P.O. Box 1867, Buffalo, NY 14240-1867
IN CANADA: P.O. Box 609, Fort Erie, Ontario L2A 5X3

Not valid to current subscribers of Harlequin American Romance books.

Want to try two free books from another line?
Call 1-800-873-8635 or visit www.morefreebooks.com.

* Terms and prices subject to change without notice. N.Y. residents add applicable sales tax. Canadian residents will be charged applicable provincial taxes and GST. Offer not valid in Quebec. This offer is limited to one order per household. All orders subject to approval. Credit or debit balances in a customer's account(s) may be offset by any other outstanding balance owed by or to the customer. Please allow 4 to 6 weeks for delivery. Offer available while quantities last.

Your Privacy: Harlequin is committed to protecting your privacy. Our Privacy Policy is available online at www.eHarlequin.com or upon request from the Reader Service. From time to time we make our lists of customers available to reputable third parties who may have a product or service of interest to you. If you would prefer we not share your name and address, please check here. ☐

HAR08R

Romantic
SUSPENSE

**Sparked by Danger,
Fueled by Passion.**

USA TODAY bestselling author

Merline Lovelace

Undercover Wife

Secret agent Mike Callahan, code name Hawkeye,
objects when he's paired with sophisticated
Gillian Ridgeway on a dangerous spy mission
to Hong Kong. Gillian has secretly been in love
with him for years, but Hawk is an overprotective
man with a wounded past that threatens to
resurface. Now the two must put their lives—
and hearts—at risk for each other.

Available October wherever books are sold.

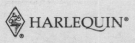

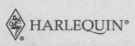

HARLEQUIN®

American ★ Romance®

COMING NEXT MONTH

#1229 HOLDING THE BABY by Margot Early
The State of Parenthood
When Leah Williams agrees to carry a child for her younger sister, Ellen, she isn't prepared when Ellen turns up pregnant! Leah, already a single mom to four-year-old Mary Grace, is left…holding the baby. And to complicate matters further, domineering Mark Logan, the donor father, wants to be a part of their child's life.

#1230 FINALLY A BRIDE by Lisa Childs
The Wedding Party
Running out on her wedding is the only way Molly McClintock can avoid making the biggest mistake of her life. But running to her childhood friend Eric South could land her in even more trouble. The returning war hero is igniting enough sparks to turn friends into lovers for life. Could that walk down the aisle be far behind?

#1231 THE INHERITED TWINS by Cathy Gillen Thacker
Made in Texas
Raising her orphaned niece and nephew and struggling to keep her Texas ranch afloat doesn't leave Claire Olander much time for relationships. Until Heath McPherson comes to Red Sage Ranch. When the gorgeous banker gets his first eyeful of the sexy, spirited single mother, it isn't only the *twins'* future he's thinking about…

#1232 ONCE UPON A THANKSGIVING by Holly Jacobs
American Dads
Between her four kids, her job and volunteering for the school's Thanksgiving pageant, Samantha Williams isn't looking for a new man in her life. But Harry Remington isn't a stranger—the interim principal was her childhood friend. Will he say goodbye at the end of his term in December…or can Samantha give him the best reason of all to stay?

www.eHarlequin.com

HARCNM0908